IN THE BEGINNING

I Am Beryl, A Chronology

Book 1

JUSTINE ORME

First Published 2018

Cover Photo: M42-HSO by NASA, Public Domain

Cover Design: Colleen Kaluza

Editor & Co-Publisher: Colleen Kaluza of www.WordWyze.nz

A catalogue record for this book is available from the National Library of New Zealand

Printed Soft-cover Edition: ISBN-13: 978-0-473-45195-0

Kindle Edition: ISBN-13: 978-0-473-45197-4

DEDICATION

For my mother Patricia,
my grandmother Ruby,
great-grandmother Martha
and great-great-grandmother Jane,
who taught me to honour and love
the Lord my God,
and gave me such a great legacy.
I stand on their shoulders.

To the only One
who can possibly fulfil
the longings in my life.
Jesus, Yeshua, the Messiah.
The Word. Son of God. Son of Man.

ACKNOWLEDGMENTS

When writing anything at all, there is always research needed, and someone has to take over the other many roles I would normally occupy. For that, I have leaned hugely on my beloved husband Stan, without whom I could not even think of writing. His support and love mean so much to me. He is truly my other half. Thank you, Darling, and thank you for your great ideas for Beryl, light sabres notwithstanding.

Cassia is a wee gem herself. Look for this name in the future. A budding palaeontologist, Cassia came up with the detailed descriptions for the dinosaurs and ancient creatures, that now no longer walk or fly on this earth. As a young teenager, Cassia is far advanced in palaeontology for her age, and I am so thankful. Love you, Cassia.

My Editor, Co-publisher and Cover Designer, Colleen of WordWyze. You are awesome. Your patience and tenacity in dealing with my sometimes 'ungrammarly' ideas, are legendary.

The most fitting of names for 2000 of my test readers is the Facebook group **Jewels Alive**. Your commitment, support, prayers, and suggestions have been invaluable. Marie, thank you for allowing me to use your group for this purpose.

Thank you to my proof-readers who took the time to laboriously go through each chapter and point out inconsistencies and errors.

For the many words of encouragement, I have had along this journey, thank you. Thank you to all who have put up with my constant - 'read this, check this, does this read properly?' You are awesome. Rosemary, Helen, Marie, Liz, Elena, Paula, Joan, Carol, Rachel, Judy, Mabel, Jan, and Fiona. There are so many who have helped, and I know I've missed some off, but I just want to say, Thank you!

Most of all – thank you to my prayer team, especially Webbles, Liz and Jenny.

In the early 1900's, a small orphanage in China, "Adullam" in the care of H. A. Baker, experienced some incredible outpourings of the Spirit of God, and more recently, Andrea and Jason Cobb's children at The Life Foundation in India, have been experiencing very similar super-natural Heavenly experiences. These two groups have paved the way for our understanding of that which has been hidden for so long. Both the Bakers and the Cobbs have overcome adversity, but have faithfully pushed through, and now we have a path they have forged, that we can follow.

Thank you. Thank you with all I have.

ENDORSEMENTS

'I Am Beryl. In the Beginning', written by Justine Orme, will open up new doors of insight into the Heavenly Kingdom and release a fresh reverence towards our eternal God. 'Beryl' is masterfully written, with fresh perspectives and insight that can only come from someone who walks closely with God. Be awakened and freshly focused!!!

Jason Cobb

The Life Foundation, Jeypore, India

It is a gift, the ability to weave life through storytelling. Justine has caught the heartbeat of a yearning I have sensed in my spirit, for illustration stories, that open the heart, weaving truth and promise into a reader's life. For the increase of those who are visionary, that we name seers. Stories create windows that God can illustrate, and awaken remembrance, causing a desire to engage and know more. These stories have layers of hope, colour, frequency, sound, and relational keys, painting on the canvas of imagination, where life is breathed. In the words of Creator, borrowed from a line within, "You will see the beauty I am weaving".

Paula Wicks

www.paulawicks.com

www.heartworks.life

'I Am Beryl' is a lovely metaphoric picture of God's love for those He has made with extravagant value and character, uncovering a clear message of how we are never disqualified from our original design. This book will encourage you to persevere through the process, to fulfill and accomplish the purposes you were so uniquely created for. Justine offers a clarion call to transcend the physical realm, and carry the light of His truth into darkness. We, as His stones, have the rare opportunity to experience His rules of engagement in the scenes of this beautiful Kingdom story. It's an exhortation to see past any pain in our journey, to realize the rewards of our completion in His call. Be inspired by the use of allegory representing each of our lives as precious stones.

Melody Paasch

Founder of Now Interpret This

Online School for Prophetic Studies

www.nowinterpretthis.org

FOREWORD

As someone who values the depth that Justine carries in the Spirit of God, I was excited to read the book you are holding.

'I Am Beryl - In the Beginning' has been divinely inspired in Justine Orme by the Spirit of the Living God. The effect the words on the pages to follow, had on me, caused me to think again about creation.

As I started to read, I found myself entering in through my imagination. One of the keys to entering the realm of the spirit is imagination, and in this book, Justine Orme takes us beyond the veil of time, space and dimension, to reveal the heart of God toward man. It shows openly, the heart of the Creator God for this planet 'earth' and how the wonder of creation affected the angelic.

In its ability to make you imagine and see for yourself, the story of Beryl touches the deep places of the heart, and opens fresh dialogue with the Creator.

Often, in reading through the Genesis account of creation, we miss what is written 'between the lines,' and this has been brought forward to engage our God-given imagination.

Justine skillfully uses one of the precious stones on Lucifer's breastplate, 'Beryl,' to tell the back-story of scripture. I love the way the story is woven, showing clearly the wonder, the love and then betrayal in the creation story and beyond, through an eyewitness, 'Beryl.'

This testimony of Beryl exposes the lies and deceit of our enemy, Satan, previously known as Lucifer. The fall of Lucifer together, with one third of the angels, caused no little consternation in a previously sinless state. The disbelief on how anyone can defy God and choose to leave His all-embracing love is evident through the pages.

With the book causing me to feel a range of emotions, to step into a place of feeling as God felt, Justine captured Beryl's story so well, and my own imagination was triggered, finding myself stopping to think things through often, through the pages.

If you are reading the Foreword to determine if you should read this book, then my answer is yes, read it, live the story through Beryl, become a partaker of the heart of God, let the story trigger in you also, the wonder of God's great love and redemption. Justine has written something special and all I can say is: enjoy the journey.

Ian W Johnson

His Amazing Glory Ministries, New Zealand

www.hagmian.com

Author of (amongst others):

His Total Provision

Heaven's Sons

The Miracles of Francis Xavier

Glory to Glory

INTRODUCTION

The idea of writing about Beryl, came about after an encounter I had with the Lord, in April 2017. He highlighted just this one word 'Beryl,' and from there came a wonderment at the awesomeness of God, how He has buried layer upon layer in the Scriptures, just there, ready for us to dig out and marvel at His hidden treasures.

Beryl is mentioned in the Bible in Ezekiel 28:13, which was speaking about Lucifer, using the analogy of the Prince of Tyrus.

"You have been in Eden, the garden of God: every precious stone was your covering, the Sardius, Topaz and the Diamond, the Beryl, the Onyx and the Jasper, the Sapphire, the Emerald and the Carbuncle, and gold. The workmanship of your tabrets and of your pipes was prepared in you in the day you were created."

This gives a picture of what Lucifer's breastplate was, with the nine stones on his garment. Every part of Scripture has meaning, and often we have to hunt for the meaning.

Proverbs 25:2, NASB says, "It is the glory of God to conceal a thing: but the honour of kings is to search out a matter."

There has been much searching out these matters in the writing of the first 'I Am Beryl' story. Even the number of stones on Lucifer's breastplate, tells a story, with nine stones prophesying Lucifer's end.

Nine means - finality and judgment, end or conclusion, not giving glory to God. In the positive, it is fruitfulness, the Number of the Holy Spirit. (from the Divinity Code. Thompson & Beale).

Every one of the stones has meaning. No one knows exactly what the stones mentioned really were, as that knowledge has been lost in antiquity. For simplicity, I have chosen the modern understanding, combined with studies in the Strong's Concordance and Lexicon. You will notice that the stones have a masculine or feminine character attached to them. Beryl is a masculine noun. All the stones are prophetic in their meaning.

You can read more in the Appendix at the back.

For we wrestle not against flesh and blood, but against principalities, against powers, against the rulers of the darkness of this world, against spiritual wickedness in high places.

— Ephesians 6:12, KJV

Brothers,

what we do in life...

echoes in eternity.

~ The Gladiator Movie

I am Beryl.
I have a secret to tell you,
if you want to listen,
for my name is older than time.
My beauty is beyond this earth
and my life has eternal consequences.
How I love being part
of the breastplate of stones!
Nine stones.
We have all pondered over – why nine?
It is known that the number
of nine has purpose,
and we rejoice at the fruitfulness
the number indicates.
I can't bear to think about
the other side of nine:
finality and judgment; end;
not giving glory to God.
Who would do that?
Who could live in His presence
and not long to pour out their love to Him?

1

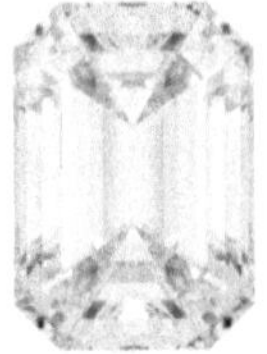

We could hear the choir gathering. The time had come for Lucifer to lead the Heavenly Host in worship. Taking a deep breath, he let it out in controlled release, the glory as he exhaled showing as motes of golden light.

Always meditative before worship, Lucifer was in deep contemplation. Checking his appearance and that he had his tambourine, we flew from our beautiful home to the Crystal Sea, where the Angels jostled into position, assembling in ranks before the darkness of the throne, as he took up his place to lead the choir.

I looked out over the angelic beings, while from the throne behind us issued flashes of lightning, voices, and peals of thunder.

We, stones, reflected fire back to the throne. My golden hue, echoing the glory flashing from the seat of God, with the blaze of lightning illuminating each of us, causing our frequencies to respond in veneration; shooting brilliant rays back to the city, high up in the North.

It is my delight as the Beryl, to walk with Lucifer, the Cherub, in his high place of office, anointed of God.

We watched, as did all the Angels, as the thunder and lightning, emanating from the dark cloud in the North City, seemed impenetrable.

With long understanding and experience, all of us in Heaven knew, that when the worship reached the darkness, the Lord God would reveal Himself to us.

The four strange creatures, who were covered in mysterious symbols and with eyes all over, appeared together with the twenty-four elders.

Silence fell. Oh, how I loved this. The awe of the stillness before the resounding time of worship. The pulsating, rich, throbbing, mellifluous silence.

Using his tambourine as a drum, beating time, Lucifer started to sing. A single note, clear and strong, his tenor voice reaching easily to the most distant plains of the Kingdom. I vibrated to the note, and the other stones on the breastplate, also took up the sound, according to our very frequency. For isn't it true, that if Heaven fell silent, even the stones would cry out?

"Glory to God," the choir sang. Bass, tenor, alto and soprano, blending effortlessly, with a top descant note soaring and intermingling through all. Higher and higher, the refrain spun, beyond even soprano.

"Holy is He.
There is none like our God.
Jehovah Sabaoth,
The Lord of Hosts."

As the choir sang, Lucifer nodded to himself, satisfied with what he was hearing.

The singers came to the end of their stanzas, and Lucifer took up the refrain,

"El Elyon"

He sang, bringing Heaven into a place of pure worship, ascending to the highest exaltation. I felt that my very self would shatter in the awe of Majesty.

Melody poured from the singers' mouths, dancing in the air; fragments of shimmering brilliance, breaking into prisms of light where the notes flowed, weaving and interweaving; the music itself, taking up the melody, as the treble clef danced closer to the thick darkness, where the crotchet and quaver joined it in a continuous unbroken glide.

"Holy, Holy, Holy.

Lord God Almighty,

Who was, and is, and is to come."

Song of praise, song of adoration, multi-faceted melodies, complex line upon line, layer upon layer of majesty, aching sweetness of pure light, penetrating the cloud surrounding the Most High. Devotion, joining with reverence, awe and nobility, phosphorescing from every being gathered in worship.

The music wove around itself; with dancing notes coming together in swirling adagio movement, grace and fluidity, to circle and form a crown above the head of God, in a crescendo of majesty. Glorious magnificence parted the darkness, revealing the Lord of Love, who sits on the throne with the Word, who is the Creator, and His Spirit, the Holy One.

And Heaven hushed. All creation, the uttermost ends of all there is, bowed in reverential awe. Trembling, worshiping, silence.

Dark purple hues shimmering to cerulean blue, lightening to violet and then bursting into glory gold.

Brilliant white light, fracturing into a multitude of luminosity.

The angels, bowing before God, appeared to be made of golden glory, such was the intensity emanating from His Majesty and Lordship.

"Holy", tore out of me. All us precious stones covering Lucifer, crying, "Holy". First, Sardius, Topaz and Diamond. Then me Beryl, alongside Onyx and Jasper, and below us, Sapphire, Emerald and Carbuncle. Set in gold. The living flame in each of us, burned brightly.

Falling on their faces, the Twenty Four Elders threw their crowns before the throne and cried,

"He alone is worthy."

The Archangels fell to their knees before His glory, and Lucifer joined his fellow Cherubim, prostrate on the Crystal Sea.

I wish I could say, that as Lucifer fell to his face, that he was graceful, but the force of the emanating radiance overcame us all, and we fell as we were, where we were.

The Great Cloud of Sons, those yet to be called the great Cloud of Witnesses, bowed low.

As the wonder and magnificence of God flowed over the worshipers, ecstasy filled each one.

No one moved. No one could move. No one wanted to move.

I wanted to stay there, drinking in and soaring on His Divinity. No one wanted to leave the presence of joy and love sweeping over them, filling and permeating every spirit.

Magnificence glistening on wings, saturating hair and covering us all in glory, until all felt we would explode and melt into Father God.

The longing, yearning to stay forever before the Great and Mighty God. The ache, should His love force ever be removed from me.

Lucifer remained on his face in the manifestation of the wonder of God. The rays of light radiating from the presence and reflecting off us stones, that were his breast plate; his garment, illuminating and mirroring the glory back to God. I felt his heart's desire well and swell, yearning passion embracing him, and so, with me.

After eons, who knew how long? The overwhelming glory cloud lifted and the Three-in-One withdrew to the City of the North.

Reluctantly, we all rose and started going back to our various places of work; Lucifer, as the chief Cherub, to the throne. The other angels cast respectful looks his way, the glory still clinging to him, enhancing his extraordinary beauty.

Angels so tall, down to really small Angels. Angels of all sizes and from all dominions in Heaven. Walking, flying. Some strolling down the wide avenues, meeting with friends and sitting under trees. Trees, whose fruit shone in glory light. Fruit of many kinds, all from the same tree.

Nodding to the angels he encountered, greeting those he knew as friends, Lucifer returned to our home, where he carefully placed the scroll of music into its niche, in the place of Many Glories, his music room. The scrolls, far from being inanimate, had life of their own, for nothing returns to the Lord God void of life.

Lucifer paused to look at himself in his mirror, and I could see my lucent reflection looking back at me. Still, the ornament of the glory of God clung to us all, illuminating the room. As he moved, and thus, we stones also, the glory oscillated around, casting bolts of fiery gleams.

Walking from the music room, and through the atrium, we flew to the holy mountain. How I loved to hear the sound of Lucifer's four wings beating in unison, strength and glory in every rush of power, as we flew towards the mountain of our God.

Moving toward the thick darkness, with the wheels-within-wheels following wherever he moved, I could feel Lucifer pondering on how resplendent he had looked, as the Kabod glory of God rested on him. I knew he had seen it reflected on the mirror of the Crystal Sea, because I had seen it. He had been made as the most beautiful and intelligent creation. He was brilliant. He knew it. Why, even the other angels told him how wonderful he was. Remiel called as he was passing, "Lucifer, no wonder your name means Morning Star. You shine."

I felt his emotions as he wondered aloud, briefly, if God remembered just how amazing he was. Jasper, next to me, shivered. I felt the other stones' pulse of tremor, 'What is this?'

2

The Cherubim are strange-looking, and if I had not worked alongside them since our creation, I am sure I would be terrified. A Cherub has the figure of man, and wheels-within-wheels that turn wherever the Cherub wants to go. There are eyes all around the rim of the wheels, which see all that is going on. But, it's the four faces that cause the most consternation: the faces of Ox, Lion, Eagle and Man.

I once heard Lucifer and some of his friends discussing the meaning of the faces. The Ox is symbolic of sacrifice. I'm not sure what there is to sacrifice for. Maybe it is one of the many mysteries of God that will be revealed in His good time. The Lion face is perhaps the most strange, for it shows violence. How can this mysterious God of love, have violence? But then, when the other stones and I were discussing this, the Eagle face is just as strange to us, for its meaning is to lacerate. I do not understand this at all.

The Man face I understand, for it is the image of He who sits on the throne. The very being of God Himself.

In covering the throne of God, Lucifer, together with his fellow Cherubim, form a guard around the throne: two above and one at each of the four sides. At times, the Lord God even rides on the cherubim.

Their constant worship shows amazement at what they see in the Lord, calling out His holiness. Always, a new and different facet of God being revealed. Throughout eternity immemorial, the Lord God of infinity.

Pausing in his worship, Lucifer looked toward the memorial stones. Sacred stones. Precious stones of living fire. The Chief Cornerstone.

His privilege was to walk up and down in the midst of the stones of fire, the altar-fire, the symbol of consecration to omnipotent God.

The fiery stones that speak of the Holiness of God Himself – that Holiness reflected in my facets, flashing with fierce light.

The presence of God manifested here so powerfully, that if we were not authorised to be here by right, the fire would consume us.

Lucifer watched, as we precious gems on his breastplate glowed, especially me, Beryl. For I mirror the exact golden glory emanating from the throne. Turning slightly, he looked for his reflection in the crowns of the Twenty-Four elders. "I really am quite dazzling. No wonder I am referred to as the 'light bringer'," he said quietly to himself.

"Conceit, Lucifer!" I was shocked, for glory belongs only to the Lord. I don't know whether Lucifer heard me.

The throne room is a place of worship; a place where we can be in the very presence of God. There is no other place I would rather be, than in the Holiness and love of the Lord and Creator.

Seven lampstands burned brilliantly, reflecting the arc of the rainbow around the throne. With flames rebounding endlessly, matching the rainbow's seven colours. The four living creatures, known as Seraphs, who are full of eyes in front and behind. Their worship swelled and filled the throne room, lauding God.

"Holy, holy, holy
is the Lord God Almighty"

The Cherubim, the Twenty Four Elders and we jewels, cried,

"HOLY, HOLY, HOLY
is the Lord God Almighty."

The essence of praise and worship, embodied in the awe and majesty, rose as incense to the throne.

I could sense that all Lucifer's previous self-conceit was forgotten, in the moment of reverence.

In a short pause, Lucifer again looking about the throne room, making sure all was in order.

"All is well, brothers," Lucifer said to the other Cherubim.

"All is well, Lucifer, our brother," they responded.

"Lucifer, your creation of worship today was regal. I felt the glory of God descend with such power, that I fell prostrate," Cherubiel told Lucifer. "Truly, I say to you, my brother, your devotion to our Lord is beyond question. I can see why the Lord God placed you in the highest order."

"My brother, you accord me with too much. It is all my devotion to my Lord, and… but, who is this that comes to the Lord God's throne room?" Lucifer broke off in the middle of his sentence, and we all looked to see who was coming.

"Hail," cried Gabriel. "Hail, Gabriel," the Cherubim called back to him.

I was very interested in this. It is not often that I get to see any of the seven Archangels, and don't often see Gabriel, for He stands in the very presence of God, waiting to be sent on his next mission. He is an angel of great might, power and strength. The Diamond hummed, for he too, was endowed with the characteristics of great strength and hardness. "Like to like, Diamond," I messaged him, and he responded that he had heard, twinkling just that little bit more.

"Gabriel! What brings you here?" Lucifer asked.

“I have brought a summons for you to attend to the Lord God. Lucifer, there are great plans afoot and He requires you to attend His presence in the city of the North.“

Of course, the stones and I were very intrigued. Why would the Lord want Lucifer to present himself before His great glory in this special mission? Weren't we already before and around the throne? What more could there be? I could feel Lucifer’s curiosity was piqued. He started to thrum with intensity, jostling us all. Sapphire looked at me, questioningly.

“I am honoured, brother, that the most High would request my presence. Do you know what He is planning?”

Gabriel considered. “It is the Lord’s pleasure to reveal His purposes in His time. We are to meet in the North, and I will send a messenger in due time, to accompany you.” And with that, Lucifer and all the rest of us had to be content.

“I am privileged, my fellow watchers, that the Lord God would take me into His confidence.” He gave a modest aside to the others who had witnessed the interaction.

“But, of course, Lucifer, you are full of wisdom, perfect beauty, the seal of perfection. So of course, our Lord would want to share His plans with you," Ophaniel said.

"The weight of His glory is heavy on me. I shall go to the Stones of Fire. I need to go and meditate on this, my brothers," and Lucifer walked away, deep in thought.

As we neared the Stones, the intensity of Holiness grew; the fire within the Stones sparkled, bounced off and echoed through our existence, fire to fire, stone to stone. Incense fell. Sacred. Set apart. The well-watered gardens shimmered with the reflection of the Stones. We all waited as Lucifer brooded. He was absently stroking me, Beryl. Would that I could impart the needed counsel to him at that time. I could feel his pensiveness.

I was startled out of my contemplation, when Lucifer suddenly set off for our home; all my brothers and sisters unnerved with the abruptness. Obviously, a conclusion had been reached, but he remained silent and we could only guess at his thoughts.

We flew over the seven mountains, three lying to the east and three to the south, with the mountain of the Holy Hill now directly behind us. The pillars of fire on the mountain of God immeasurable in their depth and height.

Abdiel, loyal Angel that he is, greeted us as we arrived, handing Lucifer a scroll that had been delivered.

As his servant, he knew Lucifer's needs and moods, and quietly led the way into the room of Many Glories, the music room where the creation of worship music took place; a place where Lucifer often ruminated, and where he now took the scroll to his work table and unrolled it. It was from Gabriel.

Immediately, Lucifer turned about with such rapidity, that we stones were set to jangling against each other. He spread his wings and took off towards the City of the Great King, the City in the North. The closer we got, the brighter the lightning, the louder the thunder, the denser the thick cloud, landing finally at the front portal.

I had thought that Gabriel had said he would send someone to accompany us! Evidently, Lucifer wasn't going to wait.

We were obviously expected.

The fierce warrior angels guarding the North, allowed us through, and Lucifer strode down the Halls of Justice, passing the seven pillars of Wisdom and Prudence, who dwell together with their handmaidens, Knowledge and Discretion, Understanding and Power. Great marble hallways with magnificent columns, stretching up, up, far up. We finally came to doors of great resplendence, created of large Pearls, luminous sheen radiating majestic light.

We stopped before the barred doors.

They opened.

Lucifer walked through and fell to his face, for the presence of the Lord Almighty was so powerful in that place, until we became accustomed to the power, that it was impossible to stay upright. Worship tore from us all, singing the richness of the Almighty and we stayed there, on our faces before the cloud of glory.

Gabriel arrived with Michael. Raphael was already waiting, and Uriel came in carrying a scroll. Abaddon, one of the Seraphim was late as always, and bowed to the others as he came in, walking over to Lucifer and kneeling beside us, to the Lord.

Whenever we encountered a Seraph, I was intrigued. They have six wings; two cover the face, two cover the feet and with two they fly. They are as strange to look at as the Cherubs. They are called Ikisat, which means serpent. Looking at a Seraph I can see the serpentine motion they make with their gauzy, almost translucent appearance. So much like the Holy

Spirit of God. Very beautiful, creatures of fire, who worship the Lord God constantly. All throughout Heaven we can hear them calling,

"Holy, Holy, Holy!"

Bang. Bang. Bang.

All stood to attention. Three times, the chief guard angel banged his staff on the ground.

Bang. Bang. Bang.

Precisely. With great authority. Announcing.

Each time the staff hit the floor, multi-coloured flashes of fire flew off it; all the intensity of our colours, the stones of office, reflecting the colours around the throne.

The King and the Word, together with the Spirit, were coming.

Overcome with the presence, the angels threw themselves on the floor crying,

"Holy, Holy, Holy,
Lord God Almighty"

And the Three-in-One passed through our midst, so we could just see the back of His garment. He seated himself in the cloud and while I made sure to look, I could not see the King clearly, just make out where He was, shrouded in Shekinah glory light, too bright to look at directly.

The Word we saw and knew. The exact representation of the Lord God. The Spirit, diaphanous soft lustres, gossamer presence of God.

Gabriel rose and bowed to the throne. "Brothers, please rise." And the assembly stood to their feet.

Without turning His back to the Lord, Gabriel the messenger, took the scroll from Uriel and unrolled it.

"A great moment of love has come from the heart of the Lord God Almighty, and you are to hear about it, to enjoy its creation. There is to be a new creation with a race to be called Man."

"Man? But that is one of our faces, Gabriel," Lucifer said in utter, dumbfounded confusion. "How can there be 'Man', when our face is the face of Man?"

"When the Word created us, He already had plans for Man, Lucifer, thus in His greatness, He showed His plan in you Cherubs. It is my enormous delight and privilege to be able to unveil this plan of the Almighty's.

"'The first stage will be to create what is called, 'The Universe'."

There was a momentary stunned silence, before a babble of questioning and discussion bounded off the walls. We, stones, were confounded. I thought Onyx was going to crack in her excitement! My own golden, yellow colour shimmered extraordinarily, so that if I weren't used to what I looked like, I think I may have blinded myself! Lucifer and Abaddon were stupefied with shock. Nothing could have prepared any of us for this development.

But oh, the God, the Three-in-One. When I dared to look at them to see how they were reacting to this disorder, the animated look of sheer excitement on their faces, was such a delight.

"ORDER!" called Gabriel. "Please, my brothers, remember where you are," for we all had forgotten in the moment of overwhelming astonishment, that we were actually on the Holy hill of Zion, where the Lord God dwells, and that we were standing before the Most High.

As the startled angels stopped talking and came to order, they looked somewhat abashed. I let out a little giggle and was frowned at by Lucifer. He did not deem my outward joy to be dignified as befit his status.

"If I may continue. As I was saying, the first plan is to create what is called, 'Universe', which will have so many different parts to it, that it will take us a long time to explore it. Solar Systems, Galaxies, something called "The Milky Way", and bright shining things called planets and stars. One of these planets, the Lord God has a special design for. It is to be inhabited by 'Man'."

"But Gabriel," Lucifer exploded. "We have the face of Man, how can there be another face of Man?"

"Brother Lucifer," Gabriel replied, a little exasperated, "I do not know the answers to these things. These are hidden things from the Almighty. He has made known to us this mystery of His will, according to His good pleasure, which He has purposed in Himself. Now, if we can get back to the agenda for this meeting."

I could feel Lucifer trembling, trying to quell his agitation. The other eight stones and I looked at each other. We had never sensed this emotion in him before, and it was troubling. As I came out of my own preoccupation, I caught Gabriel saying, "The Lord has said that the Word will be creating all this, and that He will be the Author and the Finisher."

Abaddon and Lucifer were conferring in a most agitated way. This was getting distressing. There was discord here. We had never felt discord before. What was happening?

"Brother Gabriel," Abaddon spoke to the assembly. "We do not understand what you are saying. Speak plainly, please."

Gabriel stood quietly for a moment, with his head down, as though in great contemplation. Then he looked up, directly at Lucifer. "If you had been paying attention and looking outside of your own greatness, you would know that the Word is God, and the Word has been with God since the beginning. In the beginning, was the Word and the Word was with God and the Word is God."

Nodding toward the Word, Gabriel continued. "The Word is full of grace and truth. Does that answer your questions? Now, may we please continue with the reason for our gathering here? As I was saying, the first creation will be the Universe. Universe is comprised of a never-ending complexity of what will be called stars, planets, suns, moons, galaxies and many other, as yet unnamed. For in His greatness, the Lord God is allowing Mankind to explore and name all that will be in this creation."

And the room was completely silent.

The ramifications of what was being said, slowly impinging on each angel's understanding. That there was to be another creation besides themselves, and that the Lord God was giving to the hands of Man, His own creative greatness: that of naming.

Lucifer, always the one to lead, nodded to himself and then stepping forward, bowed toward where we could see the presence of God.

"My Lord and my God, My Rock and Holy Spirit of our Lord," he started, bowing low before the great Majesty. "What is this Man, that you are mindful of him, that you will be making him?" I could hear Lucifer's voice starting to tremble. He continued, "Lord God Almighty, who was and is and is to come, we have served you faithfully. We have adored you and worshiped you. Are we no longer enough?"

Suddenly.

Out of the cloud surrounding the Holy Presence, thunder and lightning, shot a flame of liquid love, wrapping itself around Lucifer, embracing and caressing, until Lucifer could no longer stand in His presence and slowly fell.

The rumbling thunder fell to a quiet whisper. "You have known and believed the love that I have toward you. I am love, and he that dwells in love, dwells in me and I in you. You shall love the Lord your God with all your heart, and you shall have no other gods before me. I am good to all; my tender mercies are over all my works." The Word stood in front of Lucifer with such compassion in His eyes. I wanted to weep.

The room shook. The angels fell as one, face down.

"Holy, Holy, Holy,
Lord God Almighty."

No other phrase would do. There was nothing we could say in the face of this vast love.

As the delight and holiness of the passion of the Lord's love subsided, we all started to get up. This was an extraordinary experience, and in all the times I had accompanied Lucifer to the Holy Hill, there had never been anything like this.

Shakily, Gabriel got back up and looked at the scroll he was still clutching.

"Ah, back to our agenda, brothers, please compose yourselves. Now, after the creation of the Universe," and here Gabriel paused, and passed a shaking hand across his eyes. "Shall we just worship the Lord? It would be appropriate and assist us to refocus on what He is saying. Lucifer, if you would lead us, please, in a simple short song of praise."

Lucifer straightened himself, slowly recovering his poise, considering what he should sing. As he started humming, I caught the refrain and started vibrating to the melody. Carbuncle's beautiful thundering resonance perfectly intertwined with Lucifer's undulating praise.

"Come, let us sing unto the Lord,
Let us come before His presence
with thanksgiving
and make a joyful noise unto Him
with psalms,
for the Lord is a great God
and great King.
Come let us worship and bow down,

let us kneel before the Lord, our Maker."

Michael's rich baritone soared as he poured his heart before the Almighty, and Raphael, together with Uriel, interwove their voices around his. The praise drifted away, and silence reigned for a small moment.

It was enough. We had recovered our equilibrium and Gabriel was able to speak clearly again. We were ready to listen.

"As I was saying before. In this new creation of the Almighty's, He is going to begin with Universe. Inside this Universe, is going to be one special planet, which He has called 'Earth'. This is the first phase of the creation. He has invited all of Heaven to watch, as this accomplishment takes place.

"The whole of the creation will be in six parts, each part being of significance.

"After the Universe, Light will be called. Then parting of water. I realise, brothers that we do not understand just what is meant with all this, however we will watch and learn much. There is to be life on this planet in the form of which we do not know. Please, do not ask me more, because I have not been told anything further."

The Cloud of Presence moved from the room, and in awe and respect we knelt as before. The audience, for now, was over.

Gabriel paused for a moment, in honour of the Lord God, then continued. "I ask that you tell your legions and companies of angels, this plan and invite them also, to watch. I will send messengers to let you know when you should all attend. This is a marvellous thing, and I am excited at what is to happen. For now, brothers, that is all I have to say. Lucifer, if you would please stay behind. I wish to speak with you about some music." And Gabriel dismissed us all.

"Abaddon," Lucifer called, as Abaddon started to move out of the room. He turned back to Lucifer, with a questioning look on his face. "Abaddon, please come and share a meal with me later. I'll send Abdiel to tell you when it is ready."

Lucifer walked to where Gabriel was waiting.

"Brother, you wanted to see me?"

Gabriel gave a wry smile. "It's been quite an emotional meeting. I wondered if you would compose a symphony to mark this new creation. I am envisaging a piece that could be sung over the time taken for all this to take place. Your Magnum Opus. I would imagine it would involve all the frequencies of your breastplate stones, for they all have a great meaning, as you know."

Lucifer bowed to Gabriel. "My brother, it would give me great pleasure to honour our King in this way. When do you anticipate my 'Magnum Opus' will be needed?"

"The Great Creator has already started in his plans, so if you were to work on it immediately…" and Gabriel trailed off, leaving the unspoken directive.

"I am honoured Gabriel. It will be outstanding." Lucifer bowed, and we took our leave of Gabriel. We walked back down the Halls of Justice, and as we neared Wisdom, I could hear her counsel, and wondered if Lucifer would hear and understand.

"I, Wisdom, dwell together with Prudence;
I possess knowledge and discretion.
To fear the Lord is to hate evil;
I hate pride and arrogance,
Evil behaviour and perverse speech.
Counsel and sound judgment are mine
I have understanding and power."

But, I only felt him quicken his pace.

Usually, Lucifer would fly straight home. Today, however, he headed for one of the distant mountains, with a view over the Crystal Sea toward the River of Life, that flows from under the throne. He sat looking over the sea.

We all sat there. All ten of us. One Cherub and nine stones. In silence. Each in our own contemplation, meditating on the enormity of what had been revealed.

That Lucifer was troubled, would not be an exaggeration, and while we don't communicate directly, there are certain rhythms, vibrations, senses that exude from a being, which are easily discernable, and Lucifer's were very discernable to us. I felt troubled. I felt that Lucifer was not right in his soul. "Lord God," I whispered in my heart. "What is happening? Help us."

Heaving a huge sigh, Lucifer got up. "Home. Abaddon awaits his meal." And we soared off, the four wings beating rhythmically, powerfully, up down, up down, up down. Wheels-within-wheels glinting amber from the reflection of light, coming from the Holy Hill. On we flew, passing other angels going about their assignments, all eager to laud Lucifer for his beauty and creativity. Passing over the Crystal Sea and coming finally to our own home, where perhaps sense would be made from all this.

"Abdiel, we have company for our meal. Please prepare for Abaddon, and when the meal is ready, you are to go and get him. I will be in the music room." And Lucifer dragged himself through the atrium and into the room of many glories.

While I love the music room, I love the atrium even more. The square room is open with no roof. All other rooms are accessible off the atrium. There is a waterfall that cascades down over beautiful stones, that sing as the water spills onto them. The splashing of the water as it hits the stones, has been built in such an amazing way, that they create a melody; obviously, one of Lucifer's pieces. The spray from the waterfall sends droplets of moisture, watering the ferns and lilies, it is simply stunning. The seating area is on the greenest, softest, grass; deliciously cool underfoot, so all the guests would exclaim.

When Lucifer got to his music room, he took off our garment and hung it in our usual place, a place where we have full view of the room, where we can see and hear all that he does, and enjoy the music.

"Am I not enough? Does He think to replace me? What have I not done for the Lord, the Three-in-One? Always to honour and to worship!" And he stopped and paused in front of the looking glass. Perusing his beauty, looking critically at himself. "With my wisdom and understanding, I am adorned with gold and silver and precious stones. Do they really think to displace me?"

A soft knock on the door announced Abaddon. "Lucifer. It is wonderful to visit you in your home. I am honoured. But you look troubled?"

"Abaddon, thank you for coming. I feel, my friend, I can talk with you and have a good measure of what you are also feeling here.

What do you feel the Ageless One is doing? Are we no longer enough for Him? Has He tired of us and wants some different company?" Lucifer paced up and down the room, waving his arms as he articulated his feelings.

"It is most strange, Lucifer. I agree. However, surely they do know what they are doing and …"

Lucifer cut across Abaddon's reply. "But Abaddon, WE are of the first estate. It is we who were created to serve. What is happening? I feel betrayed, my friend."

Hastening to stand by Lucifer, all Abaddon could think to do, was to pat him on the back.

"Have we not served Him faithfully? Look at all I do. You hear the music I create for Him. You see the duties I perform faithfully, guarding His throne, checking the altar stones. The Holy stones of fire. What more can I do for Him? Why is He doing this? And now, NOW, I have to compose my 'Magnum Opus', according to Gabriel." Lucifer was both confused and angry.

Onyx, sitting next to me looked horrified at this outburst from Lucifer. Jasper, who was on my other side, vibrated restlessly. Who questions the Lord God! The fear of the Lord rippled through us.

"Lucifer, I am sure you do not mean what you say!" Abaddon looked shocked.

"Abaddon, believe me, this is not good. I am only saying this to you, because I can trust you. I am concerned, very concerned. I say this out of love for the Lord, you know."

"Peace, brother," Abaddon tried to soothe Lucifer. "Perhaps we should talk with Gabriel. After all, he stands before God." But, Lucifer ignored his friend.

"We must do something. I know I can trust you to follow me on this. I know that you understand; I only have the good of all angelic beings in my heart. I have to protect them. I have been wondering for a while, if the strain of governing all, has become too much for our Lord, and that the pending Creation has stretched the Three-in-One too far.

"Let us now eat, my friend Abaddon, and I will think on what must be done. We must not speak any further of this outside of this room, for it would not do for Abdiel to misunderstand my goodness. He is loyal to our Lord God, as he should be. Come now, my brother, let us go to eat."

Lucifer closed the music room door behind him, leaving us stones alone.

For a while there was silence, then I think the nine of us started talking, all at the same time. "This is terrible. What is he doing?" Jasper, the quietest of us all, burst out. "This is corruption. Never in the annals of Heaven, has there been anything like this!"

"The pride of his heart has deceived him, Jasper. All we can do is to set our face to the Lord." I was as perturbed as he.

3

Turning and pacing the room, Lucifer stopped and looked out toward his garden. Suddenly, he turned back to Abaddon. "NOW, I understand, Abaddon. Now, I know what has happened."

Since the Three-in-One had shared their dramatic revelation of the new creation, Lucifer had been seeking Abaddon out. We watched with growing disquiet, as their conversations had gone from Lucifer's initial bewilderment, with Abaddon comforting him, to gossip. And now the gossip had grown into something almost shifty, unheard of in our Heaven. Over and over, Lucifer had replayed the scene announcing Creation. Each time, he made a barely perceptible change on what had been said and done. It had grown from the joy of the creation disclosure, to Lucifer feeling that he was personally being replaced.

“Oh?” asked Abaddon.

“Of course. *Of course!”* Lucifer exclaimed.

“It’s all so self-explanatory. I have often wondered why I was so honoured to be in the Eden of God, with all the precious stones as my covering; that I am the anointed cherub who covers the throne; that I am allowed on the holy mountain of God; and I walk up and down in the midst of the stones of fire. OF COURSE!

"Abaddon, don’t you see? He has been training me for this day. For the Almighty feared that it may become too much for them to cope with, and so He put me in such a place of authority in order to assist them.”

From where I was, I saw the look of cunning on Lucifer’s face. I’d never seen that before. I didn’t recognize him for that moment, and then smoothly, he adjusted his visage and turned back to Abaddon.

For a while, Abaddon said nothing. Then turning slowly to Lucifer, he nodded. “You may be right there. It does seem to be strange.”

How far had these two gone, from completely disregarding the absolute love shown them always, to relating such greatness to a seeming inability to cope. If I thought back over the many conversations we had been privy to, I could see how the ever so slightly changing emphasis and continuing gossip, had so distorted the original meaning, that nothing of the intent was left.

"We must be careful in our planning, so as not to jolt the peace of our Heaven. We shall call on those we know who will support us, because we do know that some of the other angels are not privy to the information you and I have." Abaddon was now as duplicitous as Lucifer.

"I knew you would understand. Abaddon, I am grateful for your company and wise counsel." Lucifer's eyes had a shuttered expression, one that would not allow anyone to be able to read him.

"Now, we must use wisdom in whom we grant access to this extremely sensitive information. It would not do for the ordinary angels to know under what great strain our God is." He looked at Abaddon as though to ensure he understood.

"We must keep things as normal as possible. You know many of the angels in a better way than I do, as I am of such great stature that I have to keep myself apart from the normal angels. I shall leave it to you to compile a list of those you think will be with us."

We could still hear them talking, as Lucifer walked Abaddon to the door, through the Atrium and into the entry courtyard. Until we were finally alone.

Speechless. Overwhelmed. Confounded. Utterly, completely, confounded.

"What does he think he is doing? He can't take over. I saw the way he has been admiring himself in mirrors and glass. He has grown puffed with pride," Jasper passed his thoughts on to us.

Sardius, the beautiful ruby stone, the one whose heart is so easily seen, wailed in abject misery.

"Hush, Sardius, I'm trying to think. What are the legal ramifications of this. Are we implicated because we are part of Lucifer?" Sapphire, in his usual abrasive way, put succinctly what we were all thinking, and was always one to say exactly what he thought.

"But Sapphire, what are we going to do? We cannot be part of this," Jasper said. "Exactly my thoughts," Diamond interjected.

Topaz was losing her radiance, for if she is not cared for properly, her very shine becomes dull. The resonance of distress coming from all of us, was palpable and if any angel had come into the room, they could not have missed it.

"But we are implicated, simply because we are Lucifer's. We are his adorning. His breastplate." Diamond was very sombre.

But it was me, Beryl, whose very name means wisdom, that brought sense into this mess. "Brothers and Sisters, listen to me. I have thought about this, and while we have no option but to go where Lucifer goes, we do not need to be part of it. We must continue in our worship of the only God, the true, infallible God. We shall, in spite of all this, endure and be loyal."

4

It would be too easy to forget what had happened. Life appeared to resume its normality. Lucifer worked on his music for the new creation. How I loved to hear him singing, as he tried the words and music together, changing and rearranging the score, until it was so glorious I could weep. He would stroke each of us stones, listening to our vibrations, and listening again for the fullness of our song. Then he would hurry back to his writing table, and add that resonance into the score, working at combining the descant with the drumbeat, the rumble with the rat-a-tat, the modulations becoming perfect in its beauty. Hauntingly beautiful.

"O Lord our God
How majestic is your Name
You have set your glory
above the heavens
You have ordained praise
O Lord our God
How majestic is your Name
When I consider your Heaven,
The work of your fingers
The *thing* and the *things*
Which you have set in place."

"WHAT is he going to set in place? What *things*?" Lucifer paced and pondered, paced and wondered. "Surely I will know before this event, for I cannot complete this music, unless I am given 'inside information.' What do I put in place of 'things'? "

Had it not been for Abaddon's frequent visits, and the discussions about how Lucifer was going to help the Almighty, by taking over his throne, our days would have been complete joy, for the worship being composed.

Abdiel knocked on the music room door. Lucifer was so engaged in his composition, that he did not at first hear the knock. Abdiel knocked again, saying in a most deferential tone, "Lord Lucifer?"

Lord Lucifer, I thought? What? When did that happen?

Disorientated, Lucifer looked up from his work. "Come in, Abdiel. I was deep in thought with this music and didn't hear you knocking."

The door opened, and Abdiel came in. "My Lord Lucifer, you have a visitor. Gabriel is here. I have shown him into the Atrium. Shall I bring refreshments?"

"Ahh, yes of course, yes. Thank you, Abdiel. Please tell Gabriel I shall be with him as soon as I have tidied this music away."

Leaving the door open, Abdiel went back to the Atrium where we could hear him talking to Gabriel.

Lucifer tidied the music away and turned toward where we were hanging.

He was whispering quietly to himself. "Is this a formal visit? Should I be properly attired? Yes, I had better be prepared. Never know what he wants." And thus, Lucifer put us, his covering garment, on. As we left the music room, he shut the door behind us.

"So much secrecy," I thought, "he never used to worry about privacy."

"Gabriel, my brother. What a privilege to have you in my humble home." Lucifer exuded bonhomie and benevolence. The two angels greeted each other with an arm clasp and a kiss, as is proper.

"Abdiel has brought us refreshments. Come and sit and eat, and tell me the purpose of your kind visit." Lucifer was being most cordial and friendly.

Gabriel looked at the platter Abdiel had brought in, and reached for a persimmon. He looked speculatively at Lucifer, started to say something, but changed his mind, and took a bite of the delectable fruit instead.

If we stones didn't know what was going on, we would have thought Lucifer a charming host, but something about Gabriel's demeanour alerted us that he was not fooled.

On finishing the persimmon, Gabriel reached for the fat sweet dates and sat back, eyeing Lucifer contemplatively. "Tell me, Lucifer, my brother. Is there something bothering you? We have noticed your joy has diminished, so Michael suggested I visit you. You have not been attending to your duties at the throne. Is something amiss?"

Nine stones, having to appear passive, but crying with all our energy, "LUCIFER, confess! Drop your pride, Lucifer, and confess. If we confess, God is faithful and just to forgive us, and to cleanse us from unrighteousness."

Lucifer shifted his position slightly, so he was not face on to Gabriel.

Staring, as though entranced by the waterfall, he replied, "Ahh, Gabriel. You have me there. I'm sorry if I have not shown so much of my usual joy – my head and heart have been focused on my 'Magnum Opus.' Such an important piece, I must give it my all. I have explained to the Cherubim, that I must focus on this creation music."

Gabriel had been looking steadily at Lucifer. Could he read the falseness? Oh, how we longed to tell Gabriel, but we were not his jewels, we were Lucifer's.

"Lucifer, I am thrilled you are working so hard on this music. And I am happy that it is just your preoccupation with the music, that is making you feel distant." Rising up, Gabriel prepared to leave. "I must return to my place by our Lord. I will tell the Lord, you are engrossed in writing the score, which is why you have seemed withdrawn from our fellowship."

"Thank you, Gabriel, for your loving understanding."

Gabriel blessed our home and took his leave. As soon as he was sure Gabriel was gone, Lucifer started shouting for Abdiel, who came running. "Lord Lucifer, what is it, what is wrong?"

"Nothing is wrong, you stupid angel, just go and get Abaddon for me."

Never in all creation, in all Heaven, throughout all there is, have we heard an angel being called stupid. In shock, Abdiel stood there for a breath and then backing away, turned and ran.

Striding in anger back to the music room, Lucifer was so agitated, that he forgot to take our robe off, and as he flung himself around the room in fury, we were jostled, and our vibrations threw off distress signals. They were completely ignored. Lucifer was too far gone in anger, to notice anything except himself.

A whisper seemed to flow through the room, nothing more than a sigh in the stillness; The Ruach of God moving through what had been the place of Many Glories.

"Behold the day. Behold, it is come:
the morning has gone forth;
the rod has blossomed;
pride has budded."

"Who is that? What are you doing in my house?" Fear, a new sensation, quickly overlaid with anger, filled the space. And silence. An absence of presence, sudden lack. Void of the Presence.

Cowering in the presence of Lucifer's rage, Abdiel announced Abaddon's arrival, then quickly scuttled away. I felt anguish for him. He is such a beautiful angel. Why was he being treated in this manner?

As Abaddon came into what had been such a beautiful room, so full of the Glory of God, I saw Lucifer change.

His face had been filled with such fury, just a moment ago. It was as though I was watching him put a mask on. One that showed magnificence, benevolence and a hint of hauteur. How can one change so quickly?

"Abaddon, I am so glad you have come to me. This honour the Lord God has bestowed on me, is quite heavy and I am glad to share it with you. Come, sit with me and let us discuss what is meaningful in this matter."

How could Abaddon be so unsuspecting? Could he not see the artfulness in front of him? Oh, that I could warn him.

"Have you seen Gabriel recently?" Lucifer questioned Abaddon, watching him closely. "No? Well then, who of our hand-picked group has been talking? For Gabriel came to see me, asking questions. Someone has been talking, Abaddon. Would you know who?" Lucifer's beautiful voice became a hissing in this place, previously ordained to God.

"Perhaps it is time we all met together Lucifer, to explain to the ones whom we have chosen. You do realize that we are all carrying the burden with you." Abaddon was very cool in his response. "However, once you ascend the Lord's throne, all of Heaven will realize who we are. Is the Magnum Opus as magnificent as I know it to be?"

"Have you ever known me to create something that is not worthy of praise, Abaddon?" Lucifer considered the scroll in front of him.

"This is the best piece I have ever written, and it will crown our achievements. Now, this is how I see the lifting of our Lord's burdens taking place."

Lucifer hurried to explain, "Lest I be misunderstood, when we relieve the Lord of the burden He is carrying, that is. When the Lord God is making His new creation, we shall be as we always are, but when He has finished, that is when we shall make our move. Do you think the generals you have enlisted, are up for the task?"

"The council know their parts well, Lucifer. I see no issues at all. We are all behind you in this endeavour. It is, of course, all of Heaven's salvation we are looking at. Of course." Abaddon reiterated.

"Thank you, Abaddon, my good friend and wise brother. We will need to ensure that those we have put directly under myself, you included - which goes without me having to constantly say it - are very clear on their jurisdictions and who they have under them, as well. The structure must be sound, in order to be able to govern well. For my part, I will continue as I am, and when the time comes,

"I will ascend into Heaven,

I will sit also upon the mount
of the congregation,
in the sides of the north:
I will ascend above the heights of the clouds;
I will be like the most High."

Carbuncle, pretty Carbuncle, in the only way she could, flashed bright, a notion of light, warning, warning.

Sapphire was outraged. "This is going to be counted. There will come a reckoning."

"Sapphire," Sardius signalled silently. "We must not allow Lucifer to notice us. It will go badly. Let us show wisdom and trust the Lord God to rescue us."

As I looked back toward Lucifer and Abaddon, I saw the former beauty these two angels held, was disfigured and distorted.

"So that's what will happen." I had missed what Lucifer had been saying to Abaddon. "Good work, I look forward to seeing this all fall into place. And now, I really must finish this magnificent music, for when the music comes to an end, our reign begins. You had better go back to your position by the throne. I have been granted time to work on the composition, thus I am not missed. You will be, if you are gone too long."

Abaddon left.

Turning back to his work table, Lucifer had a smirk of satisfaction on his Man face.

"When I reign, oh yes,
then they shall worship *me*!
I will exalt my throne above the stars of God:
I will sit also upon the mount
of the congregation, in the sides of the north:
I will ascend above the heights of the clouds;
I will be like the most High.
Oh yes, I will."

5

The time for adoration to our Lord had come around again.

Lucifer carefully composed his features and became again, an Angel of light. Gone was the ugliness and distortion. We were becoming accustomed to this constant changing. He could not allow anyone to see this aberration.

Was it my imagination, or did our robe that Lucifer hastily pulled on, seem not quite as white as it had been? He seized the first music scroll in the library. No preparation, no careful rehearsing of the choir. And we flew to the Crystal Sea, the place where Heaven gathers together to praise

Almighty God. Below, I could see many Angels moving along the golden streets, all coming together to praise God, gathering on the sea of glass. Great Angels with flaming swords, together with scribe Angels, shoulder to shoulder, awaiting the presence of the Lord God.

Where previously, Lucifer had been in deep contemplation before a time of praise, there was now no preparation. Although not rehearsed, the choir, as always sang with reverence and devotion to the Almighty.

But what shame was this! Lucifer performed as though *he* were the recipient of the honour, instead of giving the glory to the Lord.

Looking intently, I was astonished that some of the choir members' robes also looked a little off-colour. A little bit dirty, a little bit grey.

We stones, at least, were comforted by the corporate worship. Jasper and Diamond were enthralled; their facets gleamed. Oh, how we all needed this time in the presence of Almighty God, and to feel the Spirit flow over us. I felt refreshed and clean again. It was as though I were being washed. Sardius, glowing ruby red, vibrated in devotion,

"Behold the Lord God.

He is incomparable."

And we all joined with her. All our various resonances, according to that which we were purposed to be, fitting together, melding harmony. Topaz regained her lustre. Emerald glistened and shone in praise. And I, if I could weep in relief, I would, for there is nothing that compares to the presence of the Lord.

It was over too soon. I just wanted to stay here in the love and glory. I did not want to go back into the tormented world of Lucifer's planning.

The presence cloud lifted; all the angelic beings finished their worship and began to dissipate, drifting back to their places of work. Lucifer, back to his music and thus, we with him.

We hung where Lucifer discarded his garment, suspended where we always did. Such a place to see and hear, and oh, if only I could sing the melody that was being woven for the Magnum Opus. Such a passionate ache hinting at great beauty. How gifted this Covering Cherub was. Without this gifting, would he be able to compose such loveliness?

"Lord Lucifer." Abdiel, obsequious in manner, hesitated at the door to the music room.

"Yes Abdiel, you wanted me?" Lucifer was magnanimous in his geniality.

"My Lord, a messenger has delivered a scroll," and handing it over, Abdiel left as fast as he could. He was not the same angel as he used to be. The joy had gone, the music in his soul crushed under the arrogance of his master.

Lucifer unrolled the scroll and read it. "FINALLY!" he shouted. "My time has come. Abdiel. Hurry! Come, we are wanted. Go and call the choir together. We are to meet in the green pastures, beside the still waters. The time of the great creation is here."

"Yes, yes, YES!" As soon as Abdiel had left, Lucifer danced around the room. "MY time to ascend MY throne. Now, Lucifer, you beautiful Cherub, stay calm, be the Angel of light you are. All is prepared, all is ready."

Donning our robe, Lucifer then gathered the music scrolls together. And for the first time in a very long duration, Lucifer flew with such joy and purpose, that I could almost have believed the changeable Cherub had changed back to what he was before. Had it not been for our slightly grey robe, the conversations of perfidy, the duplicitous breach of faith, and the knowledge of where all this was leading, I could have believed all was well.

A great crowd of angels was gathering in the meadow. Such an excited babble, as angels clustered together, in anticipation for the promised creation. Gabriel was waiting, a little apart from the rest of Heaven's population. Michael, standing off to one side, was watchful, as though looking for unrest. There had never been unrest in Heaven, so I am not sure why the Lord God would have appointed Michael as military commander. His hand was ready over his sword, eyes flickering quickly over the crowd, judging, weighing, searching.

We, with Lucifer, of course, took our place to the left of Gabriel, with the choir assembled before us.

"Angels, listen. The creation is about to begin. Our Lord and our God is about to display His greatness. The heavens declare the glory of God and the firmament shows His handwork. The heavens declare His righteousness, and all will see His glory, for God *is* judge."

Something else new. God is *judge*? Judge?

I whispered to Onyx, "What is judge?"

"I don't know Beryl, I know that Righteous Judge is part of the character of God, but who would He judge? For Justice and Holiness is part of Heaven and they reside with Wisdom."

Gabriel continued. "For His merciful kindness is great toward us: and the truth of the Lord endures forever. Praise ye the Lord."

And the tumult of angels answering, "Praise ye the Lord," rose in thunderous acclaim to the Holy Hill of the North.

Lucifer motioned to the choir, and they began on the long rehearsed Magnum Opus.

"Sing to the Lord
Proclaim this day
Declare His glory
and His marvellous deeds
For great is the Lord
and most worthy of praise
He is to be feared above all
For the Lord has made the heavens
Splendour and majesty are before Him
Strength and joy are in His dwelling place"

The light around the Holy Hill brightened.

The Word that is God, came to stand on the edge of eternity. From His palm where there had been nothing, appeared something, hazy, unformed.

I was straining to see what it was. The Godhead appeared in its entirety, working together as one; perfect harmony.

From where we all were, we could see through the edge of eternity. How is that possible? What great new thing was the Lord doing?

The choir continued in a cantata. The second person of the Spirit of God appeared again, to dance and hover over what the Lord the Word, the Creator, had in His hand. As hard as I tried to focus on this, the Spirit moved and flowed, rippled and shimmered - abstract form then back to God-like appearance.

All of Heaven erupted in beatific praise.

The Magnum Opus moved into the next phase. How long had we been here? If eternity could be measured, what length of timelessness would this be? I didn't care. I never wanted to leave.

The invisible things of He who sits on the throne, were becoming more clear; His boundless power being shown openly.

An exclamation of surprise erupted for all of us watching. Even the choir, so well trained, hesitated, eyes wide in astonishment.

For God had created heavens and a small round shape which He was holding in his hand.

We watched as He marked off the dimensions, stretched a measuring line across the round shape and took a survey of it.

There didn't appear to be any form and there was much water around the ball. It was covered in darkness. What was this secret place?

The second Person was hovering over it. The ball and its surrounds appeared formless and empty. It was a nothingness. For a very brief moment in my thinking, I wondered if, maybe, Lucifer had been correct, and I was wrong.

Thunder and lightning emitted billowing sheets of glory into the heavens. From the invisible things of He who sits on the throne, the creation of the new world was being clearly seen by us all. "Forgive me, Lord God," I cried, "I doubted you." How insidious was this thinking of Lucifer's, that even I was momentarily tainted by unbelief?

From our vantage point facing the choir, we could see all that the Lord was doing. We watched. The Lord Creator was forming and moulding and making, and all the while the Spirit person was deliberating, brooding over the mass, emanating shards of blinding light. And the Spirit of God was both before and behind.

Emerald seemed to grow in his beauty, praise pouring from him.

Then, the Lord took the little ball from His hand and placed it – just so – into the middle of the great inky blackness. Very precisely. Purposefully, seemingly in a particular position, and then fixed limits for it. The blackness was next. He stretched it and stretched it and stretched it without ending, in all directions, enormous, limitless. Some of the angels took flight to go and explore the outer reaches of the infinite black.

The choir started in the third phase of the creation music.

"Ascribe to the Lord the glory due His name
Worship the Lord in the splendour
of His holiness
Let the heavens rejoice
The Lord reigns"

And then the Lord spoke.

It was so clear. I have been in His presence many times when Lucifer guards the throne, but never have I heard this before. And I heard a voice from Heaven, as the voice of many waters, and as the voice of a great thunder.

"Light be!" Vibrating and commanding. And there was light. God and all the angels and all the stones looked, and we all saw the light was good and God pronounced it to be good. The voice of the Son came again.

"Separate the light from the darkness. Let the light be called 'day' and the darkness be called 'night.'"

What a noise. What a time. The choir had completely stopped the singing. Even Lucifer stopped and stared.

God pulled the darkness and the light apart. Just as an angel would gently part a way through a field of flowers, the Lord had used His left hand to pull the darkness and the right hand for the light. It was beautiful. Utterly fascinating. Such colour. Blending from the light brilliance into the merest hint of blue, graduating through to darkest black.

Watching intently, I saw the light as a point of convergence, until it grew, and all was light around us.

God called it Day, and after the day time, the light grew dim again until there was complete darkness, and God called that darkness, night, with paths for each light being established.

What great power is this! This is no God who is under enormous strain. This is ultimate competency. This is GOD.

Three voices blended into one, all with great power and jubilance announced, "This is good."

The choir erupted. We all joined in joyfully, and bowed in worship to Almighty God. Oh, how I wanted to just stay there in the atmosphere of the Lord. How I wanted to stay and exalt Him and praise Him! We had been starved of the presence of God, since Lucifer and Abaddon had started planning their take over. This was living waters. My soul thirsts for the Lord. We had been in a dry and thirsty land, where there was no refreshing.

When the stanza was finished, we saw that the Lord God, The Lord who is the Word and the Lord the Holy Spirit of God had withdrawn.

Gabriel was back in his place of command. "This is what our Lord calls the 'first day.' This is the start of Universe and He will call us together again for the next day. I bless you my brothers. Go now to your homes. "

Such a reverberation of excitement came from all over the meadow. Angels clustered in groups, discussing what they had witnessed. I caught snatches of conversation, where words failed to express what had taken place. Joy exploding from each face and discussion.

Lucifer dismissed the choir.

7

On a long silent journey home, I could not but reflect on all I had seen. For me, it seemed that the great glorious display of such power took just a moment, but as there is no measure of ages passing in our eternity, who knows? "Jasper, what was your favourite part?" I turned my heart to see him more clearly. Jasper rarely says much, but he is a deep thinker. "The light, Beryl. Oh, how I loved to see the light. The Lord is reflecting Himself in His new creation through the light."

I was jarred from my own reverie, by Lucifer abruptly changing course mid-flight.

Before I could even ask where we were going, my question was answered. We had arrived at Amon's house. Amon was a commanding officer, who reported directly to Michael. A leader of legions of warrior angels. While Lucifer hadn't been a frequent visitor before, he had not visited at all, since the start of his duplicity. When we had visited prior to this unsettling time, his home had always interested me, as Amon had a great number of swords and battle regalia. I had thought it unusual that an angel would have such an interest, but as he was a soldier, I supposed that was his craft.

With great fear, I realized the reason for this visit. Amon had been enlisted in Lucifer's bid for the crown.

"Ahh, Amon. How are you, my brother? What a display the Lord God put on today. Did you notice how He took so long to form this puny ball, and there were the three of them there, and then it just looked like nothing? Amon, I need to be assured that you are ready, and your legions are ready with you. This assisting of the Lord must go smoothly, so as to keep the balance of Heaven." Slyness in every syllable, as Lucifer looked at Amon.

How deep did this insurrection run?

With calculation measuring his words, Amon seemed to slide deviously past Lucifer. "But of course, My Lord. You can count on me. You have, after all, promised me Michael's position, and therefore, I have a vested interest in all of this. You cannot succeed without me, Lucifer. Don't you ever forget that!"

The menace and hatred radiating from Lucifer, caused shock waves to rush through me. Despair and anguish.

"I don't forget, Amon. Just don't you forget who I am, and what I will be." And Lucifer left in a fury.

Sullenness. Angels we met on the way, who hailed Lucifer, were ignored.

It was such relief, when Lucifer took his Breastplate off, and hung us in our place. Obviously, he was in no mood for composing worship music to the Most High.

His pride had him fast about as a chain, and violence barely concealed, covered him as a garment.

"Magnum Opus, Magnum Opus. That's all they see me as – just a tool to churn out music. Lucifer do this, sing for us, Lucifer.

"Lucifer write some music, guard the throne, check the stones, attend the Almighty. Just wait until I'm the one they all have to answer to!

"Now, Lucifer, you amazing creature. Compose yourself, it's not long now. Play your part so well, that all will be shocked at the big reveal. They'll never know, until it's too late."

He left the room slamming the door behind him. We could hear him screaming at Abdiel. "I want Abaddon, go and get Abaddon, you fool." The wheels-within-wheels clattering alongside him, jostling and bouncing, as he stomped his way through the atrium.

8

The time since the last worship, that we had attended as Lucifer's breastplate, had been a hard time of waiting. Watching Lucifer and Abaddon plot, messages being delivered from Amon and other leaders in the revolt, and the planning. What heinous acts were these!

When we were left alone in the music room, my brothers, sisters and I put our broken hearts aside and chose to praise God. Then would come the warmth and gentleness of love again. We knew that the Lord binds up the broken-hearted, and his compassion was very evident during these times. We were assured that He had not forgotten us. It gave us hope for Lucifer and the plotters, for if the Lord knew about our love for Him, surely, He would know what was happening? Maybe, He would call Lucifer to His side and gently correct him?

We all missed the joy and peace that had previously been in our home. Since the Ruach of God had blown through the music room, all presence had gone, removing all things previously known as Holy and tangible. There was a coldness in the room, and we had all noticed that Abdiel never came any closer than the doorway.

Lucifer had failed to return to his place by the throne. He had not attended the altar, nor the stones of fire.

Surely, he would be missed?

Always the excuse of writing new elements of the creation music. We knew he was not making music, but was spending this time in planning and plotting.

A courier angel arrived, announcing that the next stage to the creation was about to start, and Lucifer was of course expected to lead the choir in performing further excerpts from his Magnum Opus.

Pacing up and down in his music room, Lucifer admonished himself to hide his growing majesty, and to present the humble angel-face before the masses. "Remember to portray your humility, my beautiful Angel. Don't alarm the common angels. They won't understand that you are doing this for their good."

"How can he be so deceitful, even to himself?!" Carbuncle showed her lightning flashing sword side to us. "Oh, that he would return to virtue."

Fixing a look of benign peace and smiling at himself, he pulled our garment on, and we flew out to conduct the choir. He behaved differently on this journey, and remembered to greet other angels. In false humility, he acknowledged those around him. "Remember Abaddon's counsel." The insincerity was truly astounding.

As we arrived at the appointed place of the green meadow, I was jogged from my meditation of troubled thoughts. Well, at least I would be in the presence of my Lord, and warmed by the companionship of communal worship.

To be back in the company of those who adored our Lord, and to go back into the presence of the Lord. I was just overjoyed!

Gabriel as usual, was waiting before the throng of angels, babbles of excitement drifting across to us. He nodded at Lucifer, who reached for his tambourine, which of course, he had left on the shelf back in his music room, as the tambourine had not been used since the last stage of creation.

In irritation, he started without the clear burst of sound from the zills. "Let us all worship the Lord God."

And dutifully the choir began the practiced refrain.

I dared to look for Michael, and yes, there he was as before. Very much the leader of the host army, alert and wary. Again, I wondered just what he was wary about. Had word of the uprising met him?

And we sang to worship our Lord.

"Worship the Lord God,

In spirit and in truth

Bring honour to His holy name

Worship at His footstool

The clear notes of love the angels sing

Glory to God in the highest"

Oh, the yearning for His presence. Would I ever be free to openly love the Lord again? Would I always have to hide my heart for the malady of perverseness that had entered our serene home?

I knelt my heart in reverence. In that moment, all that I had been created to be, was in harmony with the Creator. The oscillation of all us nine stones, joined together with the heavenly worship. Wave after wave of adoration flowing.

And the Presence drew near.

My longing for Him was so great, I thought I would crack into tiny pieces, but instead my passion for Him was so immense, that a beam of pure light flowed from me directly to my Lord. And I was absolutely certain that they turned and looked at me, such love and compassion. A little smile for me on their beautiful faces. Can stones cry?

The Lord God, the Creator, moved forward to the ball.

Angels flew alone, in pairs, in groups to see and explore the firmament and the round orb that lay surrounded by water, where darkness was separated from light.

The three Persons in One. God the Father, the shimmering effervescent being of the Spirit of God, and He who is known as the Word. How they got there, I do not know. I did not see. For who knows their ways? That they were very much in one accord was obvious, for the one being becomes three and operate individually of each other, but in absolute oneness.

We were all eager to see what would happen next. The choir kept singing. Gabriel was bowed before the Lord, but Michael still had his piercing searching look.

Then came a whisper, that yet was as loud as the thunder from the throne. A small quiet voice.

Look! Look! Coming from all over, the assembled angels pointing, jostling to see better, taking flight in order to view what was happening.

And God, my one true God, stretched out their hands, the Spirit flowing around them and the Word spoke, "Let there be an expanse between the waters to separate water from water."

That voice, the same voice that sounds as many waters!

And as soon as the words were spoken, the decree went forth as waves and ripples of sound, diving straight into the middle of the assembled water. Circling around the ball, the sound waves caused the water to begin to part.

Ripples of vibrations continuing to flow, water parting, curls of waves reaching up, the power of the spoken Word, dividing and expanding, creating a space, making a clear path to appear. Around the ball, the sound waves continued to flow, forcing a pathway as it went. Higher, and deeper, forcing the water apart.

Shouts of jubilation and excitement. Awe from the angels.

I gaped, as the water above, changed form and turned into pretty, white, downy fleeces. Or at least, that is all I can find to describe them, for I had never seen anything like this before. This was again a new creation.

The fluffy white downy fleeces became a garment for the earth.

Many angels flew to investigate the white billows.

Those of us who remained with the choir, watched as they flew up to the puffy whiteness, entered into it and flew straight out the other side. It was not solid. The fluffiness appeared to be as insubstantial as trying to catch the breath or Ruach of the Spirit.

The Lord God then spoke, sounding as thunder and lightning, but soft as the petal of the flowers. "The expanse we will call sky and it is set as a vault to hold the waters below from the waters above."

Angels were flying around, examining the waters above and the waters below, the blue, blue sky, so very lovely. Sapphire was overcome. "My colour! My bright sapphire blue."

We were so busy exclaiming over this happening, that no one noticed the Lord had departed. After some time, the tumult drifted away, and the angels came back to the meadow.

Gabriel stepped forward, very much the messenger and leader. "Brothers, you have seen the awesome power of the Lord God. This creation is magnificent and beyond words. This is the second day, and you will see it marked, for there is evening and there is morning. You are free to explore. We thank Lucifer and the choir again for their exceptional worship, as befits the King of Kings."

Lucifer acknowledged Gabriel, grandly acknowledged the choir, and gave a sweeping bow to the assembled host. Onyx sighed. "Such a performance. Do you think anyone notices how false he is?"

Amon and Abaddon came over to where we were. Regally, Lucifer acknowledged them.

"Such a performance my brother. Worthy indeed of a great King." Lucifer peered intently at Amon. Was he being deliberately provocative? We could sense Lucifer debating it.

Diamond silently signalled us all, "Ssh!"

"Why, I thank you Amon, my brother and our Leader at Arms." Obviously, Lucifer had chosen to be great-hearted. "Will you both join me in my beautiful atrium to celebrate this moment? I will advise Abdiel of your visit, so he can prepare the meal." Any other angel listening, would not realise the undertone to this conversation.

Sadly, we knew it only meant more subversive planning.

9

Lucifer hadn't bothered to take our robe off when we got home. Thus, we were present, and could hear and see all that was being planned, as the three sat in the atrium.

"As I am the reigning Lord over all, I have the most wisdom. Having given this all a great deal of thought and reflection, I believe the best time for the uprising, is at the creation of 'man'. Obviously, the Lord prizes this man greatly, and it would be befitting for Him to realize that WE came before 'man' did. If we are going to take over and assist the Lord God, then I feel it is in all best interests, if it is done at the end of the creation, in order to govern all. Maybe God could then go on holiday somewhere else." And Lucifer snickered.

Ghastly, solid wall of evil. Pretty Topaz visibly lost her polish. Sapphire shot shards of his very meaning, *warning.* "There is going to be reckoning. This is being taken account of."

I noticed Abdiel hovering by the north entrance to the atrium. He had heard all that the three were planning. I wondered then, what would happen. Gathering his courage, he came into the room, bearing a platter of delicious nuts and fruits.

Lucifer flicked his finger at Abdiel and dismissed him.

I was in disbelief at this action. Did he care so little now, that in his arrogance, he felt Abdiel was of no consequence, and therefore did not bother to keep this all a secret, let alone treat his servant with respect?

Did the Lord not know what was happening? Didn't He see our suffering? Didn't He care about us?

It was wearying, listening to these conversations between Lucifer and the covert leaders.

When we were alone, the nine of us took solace in each other, and did our best to praise the Lord. But we were getting worn down and tired. Our garment, once pure brilliant white, had gone an off-white colour, then a mild grey. Now, to us, it just looked dirty. At any gathering for worship or feasting, we made a point of looking around to see how many other grey robes there were, and it was depressing.

"At least one quarter," Emerald observed. We gasped in horror. "A quarter of the angels?" Sardius was horrified. "That many?" Emerald nodded.

I was so desperate. "Can we please worship? It's all that gives me hope." I know I was not alone in this. The nine of us gathered our strength together and glorified God. Our brightness twinkled feebly, but in this act of our will and obedience, we drew strength to carry on.

There was no way out, except to remain faithful to the Lord, and trust that in His time, He would rescue us.

It appeared, that Abaddon and Amon had encouraged Lucifer to go back to his place at the throne and the burning stones, to make everything appear as before. Thus, relief followed hard on the heels of despair, with a vestige of normality and peace, when Lucifer attended to his duties as the chief Cherub.

"At least, we have the respite of the worship, when we are around the throne," remarked Topaz, who had recovered some of her shine.

The cries from the other Cherubim and Seraphim, when he returned to his duties, would have gladdened any angel's heart. "Lucifer, it is so good to see you return, brother. We have missed you. Your Magnum Opus is splendid and so befitting the King. Such glory and wonder. We praise the Almighty for your talent and your love for us." Zophiel was exuberant in his compliments.

With affected modesty, Lucifer responded, "It is only my due service to God, Zophiel. Truly, the Magnum Opus is worship fit for a King. But if you will excuse me my brothers, I must go and walk among the stones. It has been too long."

We flew to the stones. It had been such a prolonged time since we had been in this most Holy place on the mountain of God. The power of God is a tangible thing there. Only those anointed, are allowed to walk among the fire.

The holiness of this place almost melted Lucifer's hardness.

But as before, he was so habituated with self and pride, that he pushed it to one side, using the motion of his right hand, as though to physically remove something annoying. For a short while I had hoped, but hope died with that gesture.

Torment and weeping. I could not hold it back. Pretty Sardius, so full of virtue and love, did her best to soothe me. We were all very aware that it was within Lucifer's ability to cast us off, and we would lie forgotten and no longer able to join in worship with the angelic congregation, so I stifled my cries.

With a small smile on his face, Lucifer walked the stones. "I am the anointed Cherub that covers the throne. I am on the holy mountain of God and I walk up and down in the midst of the stones. I am already here and who is going to stop me from taking my place above the throne of God. Oh yes, and the Magnum Opus will be sung for me, truly fit for a king."

Did I see a sneer on his face, as he said that?

A rumbling of thunder issued from the Holy Hill. Great violence of lightning came from the throne. Hastily, Lucifer left the stones and returned to his place by the seat of sovereignty, feigning a look of humility.

It was while we were in such a time, that the word came to announce another step of creation. Jubilation and excitement emitted from all gathered within hearing of Gabriel's emissary. "Another part, what will this be?" Excitement permeated the atmosphere. We were caught up in it. In such great joy, I quite forgot my previous distress. To be back among those who truly loved the Lord God, was all I ever desired.

The Cherubs, the Seraphs, the Twenty Four Elders and those from all over Heaven came together, as a great multitude of angels congregating in the green meadow.

Gabriel stood in his usual place, with Michael again to his right and Lucifer to his left, with the choir in front.

"He who sits on the throne
and reigns forever,
And above all and around the heavens,
sits His glory."

Wonderful worship.

"All glory and power
to the Lord God almighty"

A roaring of multitudinal worship, glory; a veritable symphony of joy.

Lucifer was not pleased. "It is my job to conduct the worship. Disrespectful lot." And on that, he summoned the choir's attention and proceeded into the Magnum Opus, completely cutting across the spontaneous outpouring of praise. Carefully controlling the singers, and with great formality, he rigidly guided the singers through the pieces assigned for this day.

The Light grew brighter and stood before His creation, and the Spirit showed Himself and wove in and out between the Lord God and the creation, hovering in place, while the third Person stood alongside the Lord, seemingly solid and as real as the angels, if not more so.

How unusual though, because this third Person and the Lord God appeared to be engaged in conversation with much laughter! It had not escaped me, that thus far, all the decrees for design had been spoken by this third Person, the Word.

Then the Word spoke. He said, "Let the waters under the dome of sky, be gathered together into certain places, and let the dry land appear."

There was a deep rumbling sound that shook the ball. The waters ran away forming seas and lakes, rivers and waterfalls. Huge oceans going on forever, with great waves crashing onto shores. The water gathered into places, so that dry land appeared.

The seas boiled, as mountainous ridges pushed up with rivers rushing down their sides, eager to return from where they came.

White-capped mountain heights showed glistening, and we watched as the solid white water melted, and waterfalls formed from ledges high above the ground, raining diamond tears onto rocks on cliff faces. Angels dove in and out of the falls, splashing each other in great glee. Water ran over itself in a race to the ocean, with laughing and splashing rivulets forming great rivers.

A cracking and groaning of the land was heard, as vast areas under the ground shifted, forming valleys with peaks. Regions lifted up making great mountain ranges. Hills, and what we were to later learn are called volcanoes, shot forth pillars of fire as they were forced up from the flat plains. It was no longer just a round ball, without form and void.

Angels were swooping around the shaking ball, exploring, so fascinated with what was happening. Some flew to the mountains of fire, exclaiming in astonishment at them.

The Word spoke again. "We will call the dry land 'earth', and the gathering together of the great parts of water, we shall call 'seas'."

And Lucifer looked like one of the hills spouting forth fire. How I wanted him to fly over to the ball, so we could get a better look, but of course, he had to remain at the head of the choir. Nor would his pride allow him to.

And God said, "Let the earth put forth grass, seed producing plants, and fruit trees, each yielding its own kind of seed-bearing fruit, on the earth."

If angels' eyes could jump out of their heads, they would have. For in front of us, little green plants appeared, pop, pop, pop, pop.

Over and over and over. Everywhere the dry land emerged, green shoots appeared. The shoots grew into trees, and grass, and flowers, and herbs. All of them the same plants as we knew in Heaven. So beautiful. Flowers erupted from every niche and corner. Trees grew, and wonderful fruit hung from their branches. It seemed to take such a short bar of music, but really, none of us knew how long we were there watching.

Verdant hills reached for the sky, as lushness eradicated the barren earth.

God then reached out and took the earth ball in his hand and started it spinning, a slow spin. He tilted the ball slightly on its axis and then He and the other two with Him stood back and admired their work. As the earth rotated a half turn the Lord said, "This is evening," and the light faded away. We kept watching as the ball continued its circle and then the light grew again, and the Lord said, "This is morning." And that was the third day.

It was the next act that left every angel, who witnessed it, with mouths open. Everyone just stopped. Lucifer stopped conducting. The choir stopped singing.

God patted the Word on the back and spoke. "Well done, Son." And the Lord and His two companions left.

Lucifer tried to start singing the Magnum Opus again, but there was no joy and no pleasure in his music.

So great was the amazement at what had just transpired, that the majority didn't so much as ignore him, they just wanted to be released from their duties to go and explore this latest part of the creation, and wonder at what the Lord meant by 'Son'.

I could hear angels coming back after their explorations, highly animated and thrilled at what they had seen. "Did you see the trees?" "Did you taste the water? Some is fresh, and some is salt! Why is that?" And then, the angels who had witnessed the Lord calling someone 'son', were gesticulating at those explaining what they had seen and heard. "Son!" "Son?"

Lucifer was obviously very curious at what had happened. He freed the choir from their duties and set out to find Abaddon.

"Abaddon, we urgently need to go and study this 'earth.' Obviously, there is a lot more than we have been told. Information is being withheld and I need to know what it is. To be able to govern correctly, of course. I cannot govern what I do not know," he finished hastily.

Abaddon couldn't wait to agree. Anyone casually observing them, would have thought they were true kinsmen, not conspirators.

10

On our return to our home, Lucifer went straight to the music room. Abaddon trailed in after him. We were hung in our usual place.

"Did you notice a particular garden in the East of the earth?" Lucifer was keen on Abaddon's insight. "I saw that it was even more magnificent than any of the rest of this creation. I wonder if that is where God is going to put man?"

Abaddon considered his reply for a while. "Yes. I did notice that place. How very astute of you, Lucifer, to connect the two. Maybe we should go and spy out the land, do a reconnaissance to see what is there."

We stones, were alarmed, but also thrilled at the thought of another exploration of earth, however that was soon torn up with Lucifer's next comment. "No, I think you alone should go, Abaddon. While I would love to see what the Lord God has done there, soon enough will do. It would not be seemly for me, as the exalted one, to be seen to be all agog at this. A certain aloofness is required of a leader. Don't you agree?" Abaddon had no choice, but to agree.

It was disappointing for us. Even though the period of joy and praise during the previous incredible development of earth, had been restorative and thirst quenching, we had no choice. We were just an item of adornment for Lucifer, and he did as he wanted.

While waiting for Abaddon to return with his report of this garden, we returned to what can only be described as the new routine. Attending the throne duties, the holy stones and leading heaven in worship. We learned to recognize those who were following Lucifer. The supporters whose robes appeared dirty, giving Lucifer a knowing smile, overly familiar. My spirit was overwhelmed within me. My heart was appalled.

A breathlessly excited Abaddon returned and gave his report to Lucifer. As always, they met secretly in the music room, with the door shut. And as always, we hung in our place, in full view and hearing of the subversives. How could Lucifer and Abaddon not know we understood? Obviously, they had gone so far from the righteousness of God, that all thought of anyone disagreeing with them, did not even occur in their thinking.

"And the Lord has planted a garden eastward. There is a river that flows through the garden, that waters the area, and then it spreads out into four river heads. It is a place of absolute delight. There is a certain joy and melody to be found, when walking through the garden. It is most beautiful, Lucifer, and as you so intelligently assessed, yes, I think this is where God is going to put Man."

"Well done, Abaddon. I knew you were the right choice to share my inner thoughts and plans with. You serve me well.

"You will of course be in a place of great position when we are in our kingdom. Is there anything else of importance, that I need to know about this garden?"

Oh, the contriving and manipulation. Would Lucifer stop at nothing to get his pride fulfilled?

"Well actually there is. I was coming to that. The garden itself, is lush and beautiful. There is every type of fruiting tree and plants for food within that region, but there are two trees in particular that appear to be special. They aren't jewel encrusted, the trunks of the trees aren't made of gold, but there was something about them that made me pause. They are both in the centre of the garden, so I think we should take careful note of these. The fruit hanging off these trees looks so exquisite. The whole area feels very safe and secure. A perfect place for the Lord's new pet – Man."

Oh, how I wanted to scream at these two – STOP IT! But what notice would they take of gems, no matter how gloriously inspired by the Lord God.

"So, you recommend I take a look at this garden, do you, Abaddon?" And we, stones, watched as Abaddon gave Lucifer a sneering look, "If you dare, Lucifer!"

We felt his inward struggle, curiosity vying for control with pride, then manipulation asserting authority, looking for a way in which to turn this to his own advantage. Onyx and Jasper silently pleading with Lucifer.

How we wanted to see this garden that the Word, together with God and the Spirit of God had designed and caused to come from nothing.

He walked around behind Abaddon, who was clearly uncomfortable with not being able to see Lucifer. Peering over his shoulder and hissing into his ear, Lucifer said, “You dare me? Who are you to dare me! Yes, I will go to this garden you talk about, but only because it may well prove to be strategic in our struggle for supremacy. Don’t ever disrespect me again, Abaddon.”

And pulling our robe on, he took flight, leaving Abaddon uncomfortably alone in the music room.

We were so happy. Finally, we would see this for ourselves.

While the earth had looked small in the Creator’s hand, it was all a matter of perspective, for as we rushed towards it, the enormity of the space appeared. Not just a little ball but a giant, verdant, living creation. If Lucifer quailed at his misjudgement, he did not give into it.

Eastward, and on eastward. Around the curve of the earth, through the azure blue sky, across great mountain ranges and further east again.

Flying through the sapphire sky toward the great seas, Lucifer chose a high point on the top of a waterfall, where he could survey what lay around. The abundance of the vegetation was incredibly beautiful, and to me it provided balm. Lucifer was particularly focused on the garden he and Abaddon had talked about.

While we were happy to sit and drink it all in, Lucifer however, was using his eagle face to spy it out. We waited uneasily.

Then Emerald signalled us all, "Do you feel that vibration coming from under the earth? I am sure there are more like us here. How great is our God?" Oh, how we all wanted to burst into praise, but dared not. That would have to wait until we were, once again, alone.

He took flight again, rapidly.

"Oh! Abaddon was so right. There is something special about this place." And Lucifer came to the entrance of the garden, bouncing a little as his feet hit the ground.

We were finally here. Emerald's symbolism of prosperity blossomed in the environment. And I? I was entranced. We were all silent, in awe. Even Lucifer was reverential at the sheer beauty and peace in this place. Walking quietly, he moved toward the centre of the garden.

We, stones, were breathing in the atmosphere of a new type of life, something different, something imbued with the very presence of the Lord God, that we did not have in our own Heaven.

Lucifer emitted a barrage of anger. Such an explosion. "I sit in the seat of God. Not this puny man creation." For yes, it was indeed obvious that the Word had made this garden just for Man.

With such dissonance and jarring animosity, he shot through the trees, flying erratically, leaves and fruit being knocked off their perches. Flying up through the white, puffy clouds, and finally landing on top of one of the highest fire-spewing peaks, where the inferno reflected itself in Lucifer's red anger.

Bitterness, as gall, came sourly from his breath, and a new determination set on his once beautiful face, with a repulsive beast looking back at his own heart.

We felt the presence there of pure evil, and quailed.

11

How mercurial was this angel. After the frightening event on earth, Lucifer did his best to get himself under control, for as he often muttered to himself, there was no sense in showing his hand too soon. It would undo all the good he had done. What deviousness. What utter depravity.

Our service around the throne and the memorial stones of fire, continued as before. How could the others not see the change in Lucifer? But then, he had become the master of manipulation and sliding under any slight query that might unmask him. He was consummate at presenting himself as a brilliant glory angel;

performing his duties flawlessly, and conducting the times of worship and praise, as though his whole heart was in it.

Discouragement such as I had never known before. Where was the Lord God? In all of my existence, I had never expected God to ignore my cries. Desperately, I clung to what I knew of God. In the times we had alone, my brothers and sisters and I would feebly try to lift our hearts to the Lord, crying out to Him to save us.

"Lord God, we have run to you
for our very existence.
We cry to you Lord.
Save us Oh God,
we are worn out calling for help.
Our hearts fail us looking for you God.
But before the mountains were born
For you brought forth the whole earth
From everlasting to everlasting
You are God"

And yet there was no answer.

Diamond, the immovable one, did his best to encourage us. But the bitterness of God's seeming abandonment, allowed a riot of doubt through our thoughts.

Our eons trudged on. The endless fear of being discarded by Lucifer, and therefore never having even the crumbs of the Lord's presence at the throne room duties, brought us into silence.

The comings and goings from Lucifer's music room intensified. Abdiel withdrew further. Our robe felt contaminated.

When would the Lord hear us? Would He never rescue us? Did He not even care? Was all our knowledge of Him based on a misconception?

And yet? Yet He is God, we are not. He is the Creator. We are the created. The Lord gives. The Lord takes away. Blessed be the name of the Lord. And that was all we could cry.

12

"My Lord Lucifer, Michael wishes to speak with you. He is waiting for you in the Atrium." Abdiel announced the Archangel.

Poor Abdiel. We had done what we could to reach out to him, but he never looked up, never met Lucifer's eyes and stayed out of his way as much as possible. The way in which he was being treated was appalling, for angels were never anything but kind to each other. Until now.

Lucifer looked shocked and even frightened at the mention of Michael. Interesting. Even his name had the effect of constricting Lucifer's overbearing self-confidence.

"Please, tell Michael I shall be with him shortly." We noticed that there was no reference to refreshments.

All colour had leached out of Lucifer's face. "Get hold of yourself, Lucifer. You can do this. You are, after all, the appointed regent. Michael will have to obey you." Thus, he bolstered his confidence.

In habit of old, he put our robe on and holding his great, beautiful head high, he sashayed out into the atrium.

"Michael," he cried, throwing his arms wide as though to embrace him. "What an honour to have you visit. If I had known to expect you, I would have asked Abdiel to prepare us some fruit, but alas, I have much work to do…" and thus ingratiatingly, weaselled his way under any defences.

I looked at Abdiel, who was hovering in the background, looking on with keen interest at the meeting with the two strong angels. I messaged the other stones, "Do you think that Abdiel has been talking to Michael?" There was something about the tautness of his being, that alerted me to potential trouble. Carbuncle flashed brightly, "I think so."

As always, Michael was guarded. He considered his responses carefully before he spoke. "Greetings to you, Lucifer. I have come about a delicate matter." And before he could go any further, Lucifer cut across him.

"Michael, you know you can trust me. If the Almighty is in need of my services, I am always here as His servant." He did his best to insinuate himself with Michael.

Oh, what a fawning parasite. I could see that Michael was not fooled. "Now this should be interesting," Jasper quietly messaged us.

"No, it's not about the Lord God, Lucifer, it's about Abdiel. He has requested a transfer, so after due consideration, we have decided to grant him his desire, and he will be moved into another household. We do trust this will not inconvenience you, and you will of course understand, being a great and kind-hearted angel."

"Oh, so two can play at Lucifer's game." Quietly Sapphire remarked, with no small amount of satisfaction in his meaning.

Michael continued, "I know you will miss him, so I have arranged for one of my own staff to assist you. You are so very busy and do require support. Therefore, I have released Virtuel to be your servant, and aid you in any way you require."

How I wanted to cheer and laugh and clap and make praise to the Almighty. We could feel Lucifer struggling to remain in control. His mouth was gaping open, trying to be gracious and failing.

Michael waited for Lucifer to get himself under control and continued. "I will be assisting Abdiel to make his move easier, by carrying his personal things now. Virtuel will be of great use to you and is a wonderful servant. I shall personally miss him." And with that, Michael beckoned to Abdiel and they left the Atrium together.

We, stones, remained absolutely still and impassive.

As soon as Lucifer heard Michael and Abdiel leave the house, he went into an incredible rage. We were flung wildly, as he thrashed around, throwing things, tearing his scrolls of worship music out of their library nooks and crushing, ripping, destroying the work of ages past. Agitation threatened to claw his inner person, shredding the last vestige of Holiness.

"How dare he! How dare he treat me as inferior." The snarling, spitting fury of volatile rage, giving full birth to the superiority in the right of self. "What gives him the right to interfere in my household? He will suffer. I will personally run him through!"

Shrieking curses and blasphemy, darkness invaded that house, letting in deep forces that controlled Lucifer.

We were left bereaved, without any slight comfort from even Abdiel.

Without warning, Lucifer wheeled about, ignoring the destruction around him and took flight. His gasping breathing, laboured, as though he were suffocating.

Where now? He headed toward Abaddon's house. There was a massive stream of angels all going in the opposite direction. Confusion hit Lucifer and he slowed mid-flight, while he called out to an angel he knew. "What is going on?"

"Didn't you get the message, Lucifer? Shouldn't you be assembled with the choir by now? It's the next creation."

Momentarily paralyzed with confusion, he just stopped. How could he, of all the angels have missed the summons? He had badly miscalculated and allowed his judgment to be clouded.

Swearing to himself an oath, "This will never happen again. No angel or being will ever get the better of me again. I am the regent. I am the one chosen. I will sit in the seat of God and I will never be trounced again," Thus saying, we flew back to our home, where Lucifer hastily scurried around, finding the Magnum Opus scrolls.

Angels can move at incredible speeds. Lucifer broke all previous good-natured speed records. And we arrived at the appointed place, just a short time later.

13

Lucifer led the choir. In spite of his reticence, and lack of heart's involvement, the rest of heaven sang joyously. Our surreptitious glances at him, showed us that our joy was accompanied by his grimaces, as he struggled to appear happy. His face was taut with the effort, like something stretched tight over a frame.

What great bliss and comfort, to associate and sing with God's angels. To know that, for at least this period of creation, we were surrounded by peace, joy, and love. Regardless of Lucifer, the Lord God was here, and we were sheltered.

An aura of expectancy and anticipation overflowed onto the waiting angels.

There is a saying in the sacred tenets of Heaven, that God inhabits the praises of His people, for no sooner had we all started singing and shouting out Hallelujahs, than the Three-in-One arrived. Regardless of Lucifer's gross evil, the laws that the Holy Ones had bound themselves to, were upheld.

Oh, what great glory! The King, His Son, His Spirit, all before the Creation. What was this phase going to bring?

We soon found out.

For God said, "Let there be lights in the Universe sky to divide the day from the night and let them be for signs and for seasons, for days and years."

The Son plucked a piece of nothing and created something from it. He formed and shaped and handed it to God, who breathed life into the thing. The Spirit lingered and danced over it.

The Son Creator took the thing back from God and placed it in the black Universe. It burst into a ball of flame. Brilliant yellows and golds, reds and oranges; deepest bronzes through to brightest fire, with great tongues of flame. The shades mimicked my glow, devouring in its intensity.

"Look, look!" came from within the assembled throng. Squeals of delight from Topaz, with Carbuncle making her thundering and lightning flashes. Diamond's luminosity dazzled me.

Angels flew straight toward the ball of flame and were caught into the heat. With sparks flicking off their wings, they dove in and out, so they too, became a dance of fire. Whooping in great glee, they returned to the edge of eternity, gathering some friends to come join the frolic.

I was entranced.

And God said, "This we will call the sun, and it will govern the day, and give light and warmth to the earth."

God smiled at the Son, who nodded and took another piece of nothing, smaller than the first, and this too, he moulded and shaped. When He handed it to God, the Lord breathed on it also, but this was a gentler quieter breath. The orb glowed coolly, luminous. And the Son waited, while the Spirit hovered.

The ball of fire called the sun sat brilliantly in the universe and the earth rotated a half turn on its axis, doing a slow dance around the sun.

The sky was growing dimmer as the earth rotated and the air grew cooler.

The Lord, the one who is the Son, took the cool smaller sphere and placed that also in the Universe sky.

At once, the sky lit softly, casting long shadows onto the earth, as the sun appeared to stealthily go around the other side of the ball. One half of the earth was in sun, the other half lit with the eerie glow of the faint light from the new small, round thing.

And God said, "This we will call the moon. It will govern the night, and give a lesser light to the earth, to give the earth rest, and its pathway has been set."

The angels stopped and watched, as the sunlit part of the earth cast shadows from the trees and hills. There had never been shadows in Heaven. None of us were sure what it meant. Some braver ones decided to examine the dark outlines on the ground further, and flew to the earth.

With great delight they played with each other's shadows, jumping and trying to catch one, before the angel quickly moved and took his image with him.

The Lord God and the Lord the Son laughed in delight, to see their creation so enjoying themselves.

Such a time we had never witnessed before.

God the Father nodded at God the Son. The Son raised His right hand and flicked it hard.

Bright shining lights flung themselves all over the Universe sky. Scattering in all directions, twinkling and gleaming.

Shimmering from great distances. Many sizes and shapes. Some far, some nearer.

Lucifer just blinked. Maybe he quailed a little? This was enormous power.

The Son then moved some of the shining lights, so they were nearer or further. Closer together. Particularly, in some order. Moving more of the lights, He arrayed groups of glowing things. "We shall call these thirty-six groups, Constellations." He spoke with such delight in His voice. Over there, he put twelve of the gleaming things. "This," He said, "is the Mazzaroth, moving in their seasons. And this Mazzaroth is arranged in the shape of a crown. A crown for the Son of Man."

I felt Lucifer jolt, as the Lord the Son said 'Son of Man.'

Wide-eyed angels standing on their toes, as though to stretch in order to see better.

Then, the Word arranged some more lights. And some more, and more.

“I will guide Arcturus, the Great Bear and its cubs, and Ursa Major,” He said, all the while, continually aligning the lights. “The cords of Pleiades, the constellation of seven stars. And over here, we shall put the belt of Orion. I, alone, know the laws of the sky and how it affects the earth.”

Stepping back to admire his handiwork, The Creator Word turned to the Lord God, with a huge grin on His beautiful face. I saw they were so delighted with their workmanship and design.

And God said, “This is good. The bright sun will govern the day, and the lesser light we shall call the moon, and it shall govern the night."

"The small lights we call stars and planets, and they shall be as a reminder of my eternal power and divine nature made visible, and man shall see and wonder. For the heavens declare the glory of God, and the skies proclaim my craftsmanship.”

And God withdrew, leaving us to explore and exclaim.

How I wanted to join with the angels. I saw the moonlight dance across water, and angels walking on the silver path of the moon's reflection, across the great seas. I watched angels peering into still, still lakes, seeing their own images and being startled as another angel would rush up from deep under the sea, bursting forth to traverse one of the constellations.

A while later, for there is no measuring of time in Heaven, Gabriel, so faithful and patient, called the assembly to order.

"Brothers, this has been a most remarkable time. That which was from the beginning, which we have heard, which we have seen with our eyes, which we have looked at and our hands have touched, this we proclaim concerning the Word of life. Ever since the creation of the world, His eternal power and divine nature, invisible though they are, have been understood and seen through the things he has made. This is the fourth day of Creation."

Heaven erupted in praise and glorification of the Lord.

Everyone that is, except Lucifer, and looking around, I saw Abaddon eyeing those whose robes were grey. Their praise was superficial.

My heart, that had been filled with such joy, dropped into heaviness. The moments of great happiness were over.

It was time for Lucifer to go home, with all the evil which that spoke about. What once had been a beautiful place of joy and love, was a cold place of heaviness. A separation, which we had never felt before, had infested every corner of the home.

The wickedness, brought about through the pride of Lucifer's self-importance and glorification of his own looks, would no longer seek after the Lord God, and the Lord was not in his thoughts.

There was only deceit, lasciviousness in a lust for power, blasphemy, pride, and foolishness.

When alone, we cried to the Lord. "Our souls are in despair. We hope in God, for we shall again praise you Lord, you are the help of our countenance and our God."

But God seemed to be a long way away, and He was not answering us.

14

Our life was the coldness of the music room.

Only when Lucifer would attend to the mandatory duties at the throne, or the times of worship on the Crystal Sea, would the swamping misery lift.

We, nine stones, would cry to the Lord. It seemed He did not hear us. If He heard, then maybe, He didn't care.

Bleakness bled into a routine of nothing, with the only lightening of thought brought from the prospect of the, as yet unfinished, creation. It was all we had to look forward to and give us hope.

Lucifer continued to plot, only now it was not in our own home, as he knew Virtuel would be listening.

We made frequent journeys to visit Abaddon or Amon, and it was in one of these visits that we learned of a large meeting to be held in secret, with the top leaders of the rebellion. "There will be a strategy meeting of the leadership. Those invited will be told. The information given there, will then be passed on to each group in their command." And thus saying, Abaddon wound the meeting up.

As the angels of the grey robes departed, Lucifer asked Abaddon, Amon, Azazel, and Shemihaza to stay behind. "Oh, and you too Dagon," he called.

"Now we can get into some real planning. As we have all cleared our schedules for the purposes of this meeting, now is the time to pull all our particular strategies together. Meet me in that garden on the earth, the one in the east. You will find two trees in the centre of the garden. We will convene there." And without saying anything further, Lucifer flew off.

Because we depicted his robe of office, Lucifer made sure he was never seen without his breastplate on, in public. Such was his vanity, that he thought these emblems brought him status and power. Thus, we were present at every meeting he ever had. We were privy to all the strategy, cunning, and plotting.

It repulsed us.

We flew east toward the garden, and were treated to the magnificence of God's creation.

As the sun rose, the rays of brilliance matched those coming from the throne.

Arriving in the garden, where the entrance also faces East, Lucifer walked softly, looking around, ensuring we were alone. I didn't mind.

It was so peaceful in the garden. The trees and plants hummed with life, and I could feel the resonating vibrations of like stones from deep under the ground.

A river flowed through the garden, watering the land. The sound of the water was soothing as it made its way around, curving one way, then the next and finally splitting into four rivers.

We were the first to gather at the two trees, and Lucifer waited.

We just breathed in the peace of the place, and I gathered to my heart's storehouse, the tranquillity of the presence of God, so abundant here.

Lucifer was very quiet, while we waited for the others to arrive. Could he possibly be drinking in the presence of God? Maybe there would be a change in his heart?

Unexpectedly, he jumped up suddenly, and walked over to one of the trees. Examining it with great care, he touched the fruit, sniffed it and weighed it in his hands. A great cackle of hateful laughter ripped from him, shattering the serenity of the glade.

"Oh no, what is he doing now," wailed Topaz. "Will he also try to destroy this?"

Dagon and Amon flew in together, not bothering with the entrance to the garden, they flew overhead, crashing through the trees.

Lucifer looked at them, as though they were something to be trodden underfoot. "Is it possible for you to announce your arrival more loudly? Did I not instruct you to be discreet?"

Amon flushed, but Dagon, in his self-appointed superiority, just gave Lucifer a grin. "Well, it won't matter soon, will it, Lucifer? Then we will all have what we want."

Lucifer glared at him and stomped off scowling, but he didn't have time to throw himself into a rage, as just then, Abaddon, Azazel, and Shemihaza arrived.

"This meeting is convened. All come to order." Lucifer stood pompously, and unless the others wanted to feel as fools, we knew they also would come to attention.

"For many eons now, we have been planning. This time is now going to come to fruition, which means all of you, and your troops under you, had better be ready.

He scowled menacingly at the angels gathered before him. "You have been chosen by me to lead. You had better not let me down for this is all depending on you, your prowess in your field of authority, and your ability to lead your angelic troops. Do you understand?" He stared icily at Shemihaza.

"The plan is this," he continued, "There will be a multi-directional thrust, so that the rest of Heaven is taken by surprise. It must be coordinated to happen simultaneously.

"Abaddon, as you have the form of the Spirit of God, you are to cause the Man creation to look to us and not to God."

"Amon, your troops will surround Michael and take him captive, incarcerating him forever."

"Dagon, it is your job to get your followers to infiltrate the ordinary angels and 'persuade' them to follow us. Use whatever means you want. Destroy them if you have to."

"Shemihaza, you are to use your troops to back Amon and his legions. And Azazel, just in case you thought you could hide and come out after it is all over..." Base and foul evil poured out of Lucifer. "Azazel, I want you to take Wisdom captive. She will be mine! Are we clear?"

A murmured consent came from the leaders.

"There is no doubt at all, that God made me, I Lucifer, to rule and reign," he said, glaring ferociously at the others. "Does anyone have a problem with that? No? I thought not. Good." His voice slid with contempt.

It seemed to me, that it wouldn't have mattered, even if the others did have a problem, because Lucifer would have simply destroyed them.

Looking at the faces before us, trying vainly not to show their fear in front of him. Emotions flitting and chasing, seeking to gain control.

"And now, as to how all our efforts will look when we have completed the kingdom takeover. How this will be structured."

"My new kingdom hierarchy will be very clear. I am the king." No one dared to move, although I could see envy and vying for position, sorely tested the gathered angels' self-control.

A barbed message, not at all veiled. Brutish, relentless predators.

"I'm relieved that you all understand my position."

Amon scowled menacingly.

"Yes, Amon? Is there an issue? No?" Writhing under the barbs of hatred, Amon bowed his head, so Lucifer could no longer see his face.

The hatred for each other disconcerted us. The Lord had chosen us stones, to work together, and to see a group of angels working together for destruction, yet who would destroy each other if they could, was baffling.

Lucifer continued. "Now obviously, you have been chosen, as you are the elite."

At that statement, I could see the pride bristling all over the angels.

"Principalities," he said, "Those who govern over territory assigned to them. This is a position of rank and authority. You are all to hold one of those positions. Under you, will be those with power of delegated authority. Start looking for the obvious choices within the angels who are under your current command. They will be second only to yourselves. Then there will be rulers. I will give them power for the military training of the errant Angels, who fail to see how glorious our new kingdom is. The rest of them are to serve as you tell them, but above all, you serve me."

"Err, Lucifer, WHEN is this going to happen?" Amon was hesitant to ask, after Lucifer's spiteful comments.

"Good question, Amon," he answered smoothly. "The fact is, we don't know. It will be after the Lord God has created his Man. You will receive the information you need through the usual channels. And now, I have work to do, so that at least *I* am not discovered."

And without warning, Lucifer flew straight up through the trees, doing just that which he had so recently rebuked Amon and Dagon for doing.

We flew North, toward the Mountain of the Lord, landing finally on a craggy peak, overlooking the celestial Holy place.

Oh, the bitterness exuding from Lucifer! He, who had been so comely, so utterly beautiful, was now growing ugly, his beauty departing. Torment in his soul, showed on his face, with venomous voices shouting through his mind.

I was terrified. My last vestige of hope that the peace of the garden would reach into Lucifer's hardened heart, died on that crag.

It was nine mute stones that accompanied Lucifer back to his duties at the throne and the stones of fire, while he slotted neatly back into his role. It seemed there would be no place of joy for us in Lucifer's future.

15

There was one joy left in our days. In the suffocating atmosphere that swamped our home, there was Virtuel.

Going about his duties, he would talk with us and sing praises aloud to the Lord. We lived for those moments and joined in with him. Then the glory and radiance of the Lord God would return, and we would again, even momentarily, relish the joy of the presence. Virtuel kept our home beautiful.

Lucifer cringed, but dared not say anything.

We found it very interesting, that Virtuel seemed to understand our conversation and even talked with us. Never had Lucifer done that!

It was no surprise, when the next scroll arrived, summoning us all to the great meadow to witness the next creation.

Lucifer had long ceased working on the Magnum Opus, and now simply relied on replaying previous excerpts and replacing parts with other pieces he had written. Remembering to take the tambourine with him this time, we all went to the meadow. Our joy was to be back with the angels of God, to enter into the time of worship and to glory in His creation.

Faithful Gabriel stood facing the excited crowd. Michael seemed more on edge than ever before, and I noted some of his top ranking officers were also keeping watch.

"Brothers," Gabriel addressed the gathering, "I call you to worship. Let us give thanks to the Lord with our whole hearts. Let us recount all His wonderful deeds. Come, let us be glad and exult in Him and sing praises to the most High."

Exuberant cheers and shouts of praises rose from the throng. Lucifer took his cue and signalled to the choir to begin.

“Shout for joy to God all of Heaven
Sing the glory of His Name
Give to Him glorious praise!
Say to God, ‘How awesome are your deeds!
All of Heaven worships you
And sings praises to you
We sing praises to your Name’”

Lucifer, so proud, so puffed up with his own deceit, performed the conducting and singing as though the praises were for him. He even preened a little, as the angels started cheering and shouting. Red-faced, it was a short time before he realized that the Three-in-One was present, and that he was not the centre of the praise.

Onyx and Jasper jumped in excitement. Oh, that we had hands to clap for joy.

The choir continued their recital with the Heavenly hosts folding their voices together with the singers while those playing in the orchestra thrummed and strummed and wove praise in harmony blending around the notes, weaving highest praises.

The pre-eminence of the glory of the Lord abounded toward us bringing the delight of His presence.

One by one and group by group, the angels bowed in reverence. Hot tears poured through my heart, for I was in His majestic company.

At that moment, I didn't remember Lucifer's hatred, for the ocean of love pouring from my heart towards the Lord, diminished past pain.

All of Heaven was waiting for the Word, for from Him and through Him were all things made. In His hand are the depths of the earth, and the mountain peaks, for they belong to Him. The sea is His, for He made it, and His hands formed the dry land.

The Word and the Lord God, with the Spirit of God, moved as one, and God said, "Let the waters teem abundantly with living creatures."

Angels rushed to the edge of eternity, jostling for a better view. Many took flight to look down on what was happening; a gambol of angels.

As the Word spoke, the Spirit of the Lord God leaped high and caught the quiet thunder of decree. Moving swiftly, He carried the words, flying into the water and releasing the sound of life.

Churning, splashing, jumping. Silver fins appeared attached to large shiny backs, the colour of the moon.

Beautiful, friendly faces leaping high out of the water, scudding along backwards on their tails, laughing in joy at the presence of the Lord.

So many different kinds of creatures. Creatures with eight waving appendages, huge creatures, little wee ones. All appeared at the sound of the edict, flapping flippers in joy.

The Word moved and stood on the water, telling the sea creatures, "Be fruitful and multiply and fill the water in the seas, the lakes, the rivers and the oceans."

Such a boisterous cry of praises and delight from all these new creations. I so wanted Lucifer to abandon his place, and have a look at this delight, but of course, he was unbending, and would not.

I listened to angels, who had delved deep into the waters to look at and talk to these new ones. "Did you see that enormous one, with the long neck and small round head. It was comical. Such a round body and a short tail. Four flippers!" said one angel, while another chattering excitedly, talked about sea creatures that went on both land and water, waddled on their back feet and clapped their flippers together, gakkering and peeping, honking at each other. "Yes, but did you go deep and see all the coloured ones? Swimming around, in and out, and there are plants down there! I didn't know the Lord had created sea plants!" Astonishment and excitement babbled as a symphony.

The angels and the sea creatures raised a tumult of praises, which melded together as the waves washed onto the shore.

I looked at the Word, who had a delighted smile on His face. He looked at the Lord God, and then the Spirit of God soared up from the depths and went back to God, where the Son joined them.

All Heaven watched a riot of brilliantly coloured splashing, with sea creatures celebrating by leaping high, and jumping. A loud barking roar from large ones that waddled from the sea to the land, as they plonked themselves on rocks in the sunshine, rivulets running off their fur coats.

A great leviathan joined other enormous sea creatures.

The creatures that scudded backward on their tails, gave trills and squeaks, while the enormous ones that leapt high and landed with great splashes, slapped the water with their fins, calling with clicks, whistles and pulsing. It was a joyous cacophony! Leviathan slid in and out of the water, wary and watching.

One of the enormous ones gave a great vault; high out of the water and landing with a big splash, diving down again, while slapping his wedge of a tail hard on the water.

Fish leaping, gathering themselves into groups of common types, cavorting and splashing.

Four-legged creatures, with hard shells on their backs, lumbered out of the water to sun themselves on the warm sands of beaches.

"This is good," the Son exclaimed.

Emerald, Sapphire, and Topaz sparkled, imitating the colour of the water, in a display of radiant brilliance.

I just sighed in contentment. To be where my Lord was, to see all these happenings. Was there anything better?

Sneaking a look at Lucifer, I was dispirited at the bitterness in his eyes. He couldn't even enjoy this.

I gradually became aware that the Son, He who is the Word, was commanding attention again.

Was there going to be more?

He said, "Let birds fly above the earth, across the expanse of the sky."

Birds! What are birds? I couldn't wait to see what He would do next. How He could create a whole universe and all in it, simply by speaking. Something out of nothing?

The Word stooped, gathering a handful of dirt from the earth, and held it in his hands. He whispered, "Birds, be!" A fluttering sound, overlaid with a whooshing, the Lord opened His hands and where there had been dirt, was now a myriad of living things. Tiny little ones, and enormously large things. All had feathers and most had wings. Fantastically coloured. Cheeky little ones and immense birds with considerable wingspans. Ones I heard called 'eagles,' and they had the face of an eagle, the same as the Cherubs wear.

These things the Lord had called birds, flew above Him, circling around, and some came back in to land on His arms.

What a chit-chat of noise, with a flapping of wings.

A bird, that was as big as a warrior angel, was wheeling above the Lord, a screeling cry emitting from its huge mouth.

Grey and brown body, with a short fuzz covering, with a long pale yellow bill and a comb on its head, the colour of the deepest ocean. Its wings didn't have feathers, but were more like what the angel's sandals were made of.

We were so intrigued with this bird creature.

A collective gasp came from the angels, as they discussed amongst themselves, comparing their wings with the wings of these 'birds'.

Angels soared into the blue sky, flying amongst the birds, talking to them, comparing wingspans, racing bird to angel. Soaring high and higher, then diving straight down, kersplash into the water, startling the fish below.

Brilliant blue and yellow birds flitted around with little brown birds. Birds with great combs on their heads, others with the most enormous tails, that when fanned out, mimicked the eyes all over the Cherub's wheels-within-wheels.

Shouts announced seabirds with great spoons of beaks. Birds settled on the sea, rocking gently as the water lapped around them. Strange-looking pink ones balanced on one leg in the shallows.

Birds that nested up high, to the forests and the plains, the marshes, and the rain forests.

Seabirds. Land birds. Birds that nested behind waterfalls. Birds wheeling, diving, screeling.

"Look!" Topaz was so excited, she forgot to be discreet.

We all looked in the direction she was indicating.

Birds all very similar, but different in height and colouring, were waddling on two legs up, out of the sea. They had wing-like protuberances, which we supposed were arms, and they used those to steady themselves as they shuffled from water to land, only to find a rock and then dive straight back into the water, swimming like the fish. Were they birds or were they fish?

God laughed at the antics of the birds and the angels.

A tiny bird, whose wings hummed as it flew, reflected every colour of us stones. Oh, the Lord was so wonderful. He reflected His very essence in His creation, again and again, mirroring Himself in all He made, with colour and effect, noise, joy, and love.

Every colour we knew in Heaven, was present and repeated in these birds.

What riotous, cosmic dancers they were!

"Now, be fruitful and increase on the earth, my pretty ones. Inhabit every corner of the earth, from the plains to the highest mountain peaks." And as the Word finished speaking, the birds did a final swoop around Him, forming a crown above His head and left, flying into the skies.

"Let there be storehouses for snow and hail, rain and ice." And it was so. God saw this all and said it was good.

Silence fell and blossomed, and the glory increased.

We waited. We waited and watched, as leaves fell from trees and the air cooled. We waited and watched as the tops of mountains grew white.

As the white fell on the mountain tops, some drifted down toward the ground. Some of the angels flew down to inspect this more closely, and caught flakes of the white in their hands. They excitedly compared them with each other. Not one flake was the same as the next. That the Lord God was so magnificent, that He could create so many, many of these white flakes and yet each one of them was unique!

We waited and watched as the white topped mountains melted, as the air grew warmer again, and the trees budded with little green tips. The birds had young and grew in number.

"These are Seasons," Gabriel announced. Angels bowed in awe before the Lord God.

It was evening. The earth moved around the sun. The shadows grew long, and the moon showed its beauty. Stars sang in the heavens and still, we waited before the glorious Ones. As the earth rotated, the moon receded, and the sun came again.

It was morning.

When we all straightened, the Son raised His right hand in blessing. In silent adoration, we watched as God left. Gabriel glowed for he lives before the very Ones whom we worship.

"This is the fifth day of the creation of this Universe and earth," Gabriel said.

We were free to either explore these sea creatures and birds further, or go home. Lucifer went home and of course, that meant we nine stones did, as well.

I was quiet in wonderment. The peace of this overwhelming event welled in my heart.

"Ridiculous sycophants." I hadn't noticed Abaddon coming up to Lucifer, and his words jarred; destroying the soft silence.

"Brother," Lucifer was being at his most gracious, "shall we dine together?"

Diamond uttered a quiet groan. That meant listening to the conspiracy, yet again.

Dread took over from awe. When will this horror end!

16

"WHEN Lucifer?! Just when are you planning on this happening?" Abaddon asked, as he came striding into our house, confronting Lucifer in a loud voice.

Lucifer went rigid, his eyes blazing with fury. "Use discretion, Abaddon! Don't you ever come into my home in that manner again! I am Regent! Not you! I shall say when something is going to happen. Besides, you know that Michael has planted Virtuel here as a spy!" he hissed. "It's as well for us both, that he has not yet returned from the creation event. Let me get out of this garment, and then I shall organize a meal."

Shrugging our covering off, he hung us up in the music room, leaving again and shutting the door behind him.

"We don't need to be subjected to his deceit yet again. I am very relieved he left us here." Onyx remarked, who was normally very quiet. He wasn't the only distressed one.

"My brothers and sisters. Is there anything we should be doing that we aren't?" I asked, as I was now getting angry.

Why hadn't the Lord God pulled Lucifer, Abaddon, Amon and all the rest of the rebellious ones back into line? Did He not care?

"If I have to listen to this anymore, regardless of protocol, I am going to explode into great schisms of outrage!" I said, getting exasperated and bitter.

"Oh, what's the use. God is not listening to us. I have tried hard to keep my heart toward Him. I have done all I can, and He is simply deaf or doesn't care. Or maybe," I said angrily, "maybe He is simply a liar." And on that, I broke into a torrent of weeping. Limp and exhausted with disappointment, I had never felt so hopeless.

The other stones remained silent through my outburst of pain. No one knew what to say or do. It went against all of Heaven's principles to speak in this manner. There had never been a need to, before.

This heavy atmosphere was becoming our new normal.

"Beryl, my lovely brother stone," Sardius said so gently, "we know that hope deferred, makes the heart sick. And yet, we choose to trust the Lord." She started singing softly, her red heart of sacrifice glowing. Topaz joined in, creating harmony.

"Hear my prayer, O Lord,
and let my cry come unto you
Hide not your face from me in the day,
when I am in trouble
Incline your ear to me
In the day when I call,
answer me speedily
By reason of the voice of my groaning
My heart is smitten and withered
Hear our cry, O God,
Attend unto our prayer
Our hearts are overwhelmed

You are a shelter for us

A strong tower

We will trust in your cover

So, we will sing praise to your name

forever

That daily, we may perform

our offerings to your Name"

Their praises broke off the frustration and despondency that clung to us all.

"I'm sorry. I allowed myself to become downhearted. In taking my hope off the Lord and looking around at what was happening, it had dragged me into Lucifer's vortex. Forgive me. The Lord is my stronghold. He is my rock of refuge. In Him will I trust. Regardless, my fellow stones, I will trust Him." I was contrite and begged the Lord's forgiveness. But I was struggling. I was failing in this trial.

We could not understand why God had allowed this to happen, and even more, why He had allowed it to go on for so long.

So, we just hung there, on our garment, on the peg in the music room. Mute emptiness.

17

Loud noise drifted through to our consciousness. Diamond signalled us all: "What's happening?" We strained to hear. What a commotion. Was Lucifer throwing things again? No. It was shouting.

"Lucifer, Lucifer are you there?" It was Gabriel's emissary. "LUCIFER."

"I'm here, there is no need to screech Adlai, I am right here. I was in the garden meditating, thus did not hear you. Now, what is it you want?"

"Meditating!" Emerald snorted. "More likely imagining his renegade dream."

"Lucifer, get your breastplate, the Lord God is about to start the final stage of His glorious creation, and you are required to perform the most magnificent part, being the climax of your Magnum Opus. You have been working on it for so long. It is going to be wonderful." Adlai was so excited. We could feel the vibrations of joy. "I have to go now and alert the others. See you at the meadow."

"That means we will be back in the presence of the Lord," I messaged the others. Joy, joy, joy.

As he rushed in to put us on and get the tambourine, Lucifer was looking as grey as our garment. Were the ramifications of his actions finally getting through to him?

"How am I going to get a message to the others? Who shall I send.?" He was in a flurry of anxiety. Flying chaotically, he was telling any grey robed angel he came across, "Find Amon. Find Abaddon. Tell them to come to me at the meadow, immediately."

We could hear the desperation in his voice. Was this going to be it, then? Was this where our lives would diverge from that of the Creator? God help us.

On arriving at the great meadow, Lucifer took on the façade of an angel of great light and beauty. But there was an iciness about him that belied his appearance.

Waiting uneasily, he was rattling his tambourine, chittle, chittle, chittle; a jangling discordance with no artistry in it. We knew, and he knew, that he had not written the ending to the Magnum Opus. There was no climactic ending to the work. He had not done anything to the script for a very long time.

As the angelic choir gathered in place before him, we could see Lucifer struggling to work out what to do and how to make it appear as though he had created something that would crown the end of the Lord God's universe work.

Speaking with the various segments of the choir, he quickly directed what and how they would sing. We saw that some of them had grey robes on and the ones that didn't, were looking at Lucifer quizzically. He waited uneasily.

"Finally, Abaddon!" Lucifer's voice told us he was ready to direct more than just music.

"It's time, Abaddon. All our work is finally going to come to fruition. Now, listen very carefully. Find Dagon. Tell him to get his minions to move to the outer edge of the gathering here. They are to arrange themselves, so they are encircling the field. Amon and his troops are to take Michael, while the minions take care of the rest. Shemihaza is to use his forces and powers to back Amon with his minions, and Azazel must capture Wisdom. You, Abaddon, are to go straight to the garden and get this man creature. But wait for my signal! Do NOT move before seeing my signal."

"And just what might your signal be, Lucifer, my dear leader?" Abaddon's scathing tone was lost on Lucifer, who was full of his own glory.

"Wait for my signal." The ice in his voice jarred with his beauty. "I will fly straight up. You won't miss it, because it will be abrupt, and I will issue a war cry at the same time. From my ascent up, I will then ascend the throne. Do you like that witticism, my friend?" He chortled in evil glee.

Abaddon simply nodded and moved off, I assumed, to alert the rest of the dirty-robed traitors.

In desperation, I signalled Diamond. He quietly just let me know, there is nothing we can do. Our hearts' loyalty lies with the King, but the King gave us to Lucifer as his covering garment. Our Heavenly loyalty had us trapped.

All became still and quiet, and Heaven bowed. We waited in the presence of the Lord God, the

Son, and the Spirit of the Living God. Though he had set his heart against the Lord, even Lucifer was overwhelmed, and forced to kneel in the Holy Presence.

The Holiness grew and pulsed, drawing in all and everything around the heavens. The Son, being the radiance of God's glory and the exact representation of His being, glowed with his face as the sun shining in all its brilliance.

"Holy," came from over here and "Holy," from over there. As though someone had taken a handful of sand, and thrown it up in the air, the Ruach of God caught it, so where the sand landed, a smattering of "Holy," "Holy," "Holy" swelled, burst, and flew from around the assembled angels, gathering momentum until all took up the chorus:

"Holy, Holy, Holy,
Lord God Almighty
Who was, and is, and is to come"

Kneeling, then face down. One by one, the angels melted in adoration of the Holy Ones.

Joy pouring over all; unspeakable, unutterable beauty.

My golden aspect caught the glory, rebounding depths of majesty to my Lord.

Multi-hued flashes of fire, intense in my returning, unending glory, wave to glorious wave.

The Lord of Love's light shone through me and bounced back to His heart, His beloved face reflected in my facets.

I hungered for these times, for I knew, should Lucifer succeed, this would be one of the last times I would have the privilege of the presence of God, reflecting off my very self.

Quietly, Lucifer started singing a piece of the Magnum Opus. As arranged, the choir joined in. The Holiness stayed around us all.

The Three-in-One stood together. Daring to look, I saw the Son, dressed in a robe reaching down to His feet, and with a golden sash around His chest. My colours echoed His eyes, which were as blazing fire. His dress showed that this time of creation had reached its pinnacle. Would this be the point in which the corrupt angels would show themselves?

"My stones, could this be the time? What will happen to us?" I silently messaged the others.

"Will we be forced to stay with Lucifer!?" Closed up agony.

"Remember brothers and sisters, we will worship the Lord God, no matter what." Sardius was such an encourager.

"Yes," I thought, "Yes I will." And resolutely turned my face to the Lord God.

Absolute stillness paused the choir, and the Word spoke. "Let the land produce living creatures according to their kinds: livestock, creatures that move along the ground, and wild animals, each according to its kind."

As before, when he had made the birds, the Son stooped to get some dirt. This time, instead of forming in his hands, he sat on the ground and moulded the earth creating so many different shapes.

Lucifer motioned for the choir to begin again. He started a hymn of such aching sweetness.

I was startled, for I had never heard this one before.

The choir following, with their voices rolling and mingling with his. And then, I looked at Lucifer, as the other eight stones did, and we saw a thaw in his hardness. Oh, God, please let it continue.

"Blessed are you, Lord God
For you are Creator of
Heaven and Earth
All things come from your hands
He is before all things,
And in Him all things hold together"

The Lord God knelt in the dirt with the Son, and the Spirit was over and through all. Together they worked, moulding, shaping. Forging a whole new type of creation that none of us had ever seen before. Laughing, the three continued in their work. To me, looking on, they appeared to be having a competition! For some of the beings were very strange to look at. Groups of creatures were emerging, solid in the clay from which they were made. From the very hands of God.

The angels were watching intently.

I could hear exclamations from throughout the field, of "Look, He has created something that looks like me!" And as I looked, I saw it was so.

For the Lord had taken the image of some of His angelic creation, and made it as a creature of the earth.

Beautiful, winged beings. Wings that reflected the sun overhead and became a poem of colour. Two wings. Four wings and a furry body to which the wings were attached. Every colour that was in Heaven was in these winged ones. Every shade of the blue sky and the deepest blue ocean. Every shade of the brilliance of the sun, to the leaves as they fell when the seasons turned. White, brown, yellow, orange, pink, purple, blue, and green.

So many I could not count. It was the beauty of the Spirit of God enmeshed in the gauze of their wings.

God blew on these beautiful mud ones and as His breath of life reached them, they took on life of their own.

Stretching and trying out their wings, they gracefully fluttered off the earth, proving their wings in a kaleidoscope of colour.

The Son smiled at them and spoke. "Now go, and settle all over the earth. Be fruitful and multiply in numbers."

Dipping and swirling they danced before the Lord God, the Son and the Spirit of God, and then flew out in all directions; myriads like flying flowers.

The choir broke into a torrent of delight:

"Hallelujah

Hallelujah

Glory be to the Lord God on High"

All nine of us stones, laughed in glee, for look, our colours were also in these flying ones. This was not just a poem of colour, but poetry in motion.

Turning back to what God was doing, the angels had to crowd in closer, for the Holy ones were making the tiniest creatures. The Lord motioned to what they were working on. "All creeping things." And these were tiny little creatures.

Most of them were of dull colours, browns and shiny blacks, sombre deep charcoals, and some threw splashes of brightest hues. Some had wings. Some used their many legs to crawl along the ground. Six and eight legs. Some had a huge number of legs. There were tiny ones, and then we saw bigger ones. Nearly all had probing fragile things protruding from their heads. They were all very strange to look at. As the Lord released them with His breath of life, a few of the angels dashed to investigate and talk with these creatures.

I waited until I could hear drifts of conversation coming back from the earth, to where we were on the edge of eternity. "They are called insects." From one quarter. "Most of them go through cycles of life, an egg which hatches to a larva, which then grows into their own type. How amazing!" Clutches of angels were discussing the new lives. "Some only crawl and when they come from the 'larva' stage, they grow wings and can fly like us."

"Lucifer, is it time yet?" Dagon had come right up to Lucifer openly, in front of all the host. "God must be almost finished making His creation. When will you give the signal?"

Where Lucifer had softened before, his face now held contempt.

"Is that the best He can do with His creation? No wonder I need to take over. Dagon, my instructions are clear. Wait until you see the signal."

He whispered oh so quietly, but we heard, and Topaz's heart wilted.

As Dagon slipped away, I turned quickly when I heard the Son laughing out loud. "What? What is so funny?" And then I saw and the whole of

Heaven was in riotous laughter, for the Lord God, the Son and the Spirit of God, appeared to be in a competition to see who could create the strangest looking beings.

It was a wild array of shapes being set out in groups from very large to very small. The Lord spoke. "The land produces living creatures according to their kinds: the livestock." And He motioned to one group of clay creatures. "Wild animals."

I looked at the group called 'livestock.' A four-legged animal with large soft eyes stood awaiting the Ruach breath of God.

There were several of these animals, but all slightly different. The first two had straight backs, and a tail. The tail appeared small in comparison to the size of the beast. Both were covered in a hide of hair. They had a horn growing out of either side of their head.

From the underside of one, hung a pendulous bag with four things that looked like fingers. The other beast was the same, but without the bag. In its place was the organ that indicated the male of the species. This then made a pair, male and female, representing two sides of the Lord God. How clever!

The next group of two looked very similar to the first except these ones had a humped ridge flowing up to their heads, which were covered in shaggy hair. These also had horns, although larger than the first two animals.

The Three-in-One continued working on creatures like the first ones, and then moved onto a smaller animal within the group, called livestock. Again, they had four legs and again, the male and female of the pair had similar identifiers. However, these ones were covered in a white woolly coat. Only the male of the pair had horns.

So many to look at. Not being able to see them all, I looked next at the creatures the Lord had called 'Wild Animals.' Now I saw why the angels had been laughing so uproariously. For there, in the clay, were the strangest looking things I had ever seen.

A four-legged animal with a tail that was as long as its body, and an elongated head that was almost the same size as the tail. The tail was shaggy with long hair, while the head had short hair. The nose – well, if an angel had a nose that shape, he would be constantly laughed at.

There were huge animals, two kinds that looked similar, but were different. One pair had legs like trees and a large mobile nose from underneath, on either side of which grew two great horns. The other pair looked very similar, except they were covered in a hide of long hair, and their horns were a lot bigger.

Quickly, before an angel got in the way of my view, I looked at others. Being created, was a beautiful wraith-like being. Gasps and laughter from the Seraphim, "They look just like us!"

And another was being created. Even bigger than the others, this creature was simply enormous. With four stumpy legs, it had diamond shaped plates on its back ridge, and at the end of its tail were four spikes. The ridges were brilliant reds and oranges on a muddy brown body.

What a magnificent time! The vast array of beasts and flying creatures; the fish in the sea and the birds in the air; this was a kaleidoscope of imagination.

The choir was staggering along, trying to make the most of Lucifer's unfinished Magnum Opus, which was interspersed with older pieces of music. But no one seemed to notice. We were all too focused on what the Godhead were doing.

Onyx suddenly signalled for us to pay attention.

Lucifer became aware of the change of atmosphere. He looked to Gabriel for guidance, who did not acknowledge him. The music faltered to a halt.

I dared to look at Michael. He was scanning the crowd, and I could see his warriors moving to the outer edges of the gathering, getting closer to those in grey robes. Would this be it then?

The Son stood, finished in His work. The Spirit of God hovered over all the array of animals while the Lord God knelt before the amassed clay shapes. The look in His eyes. The love He bore these pieces of their making. And then He breathed His breath of life over all.

As though waking from a long and deep sleep, the creatures took life, from the tiniest to the largest. They breathed and moved. The joy of life in every action as they looked around, and took stock of where they were.

God blessed them and said, "This is good!"

Gabriel looked at Lucifer.

Panic rippled through our breastplate. Choking constriction.

"Please sing, Lucifer. Sing the crescendo." Gabriel's instructions brought immense relief. For now, we were safe.

Lucifer sang. The choir joined in the refrain.

"Blessed be the name of the Lord.
From the rising of the sun,
unto the going down of the same,
The Lord's name is to be praised.
The Lord is high above all,
and His glory above the heavens."

It was the symphony of Creation. Praises rising together with the waves on the seashore. The birds sang in the most joyous twittering and tweeting. The fish who scud backwards on their tails, sang with whistles and trills, while the huge ocean creatures pulsed their calls in time with Lucifer's tambourine.

All of creation, both heavenly and of this earth came to a crescendo together with the choir, the pinnacle of praise to the Highest.

And then, silence moved in underneath, while the last notes were yet falling off.

Absolute silence.

"Let us make mankind in our image, in our likeness, so that they may rule over the fish in the sea and the birds in the sky, over the livestock and all the wild animals, and over all the creatures that move along the ground," the Word decreed.

"Ssssss," escaped from Lucifer. His whole being was stiff, eyes bulging and neck cords rigid. We sensed the roiling anger under the surface. "They are going to rule all!" Such hatred he had for this mankind.

From the dust of the earth, the Lord God fashioned man in His own image. Moulding and shaping. Forming a new being. Even while the man-shape was imperfect and unfinished, all his inner parts were inscribed, engraved and written down. Registered and decreed.

The Lord called out the man's plan and purpose, while a scribe captured the words and wrote in the Book of Destiny. Letters of instruction, commissions, and decrees. His genealogical register and a book of poems the Lord sang over the man. The book of records in which his life would be recounted and written.

We watched in astonishment, as God reached into His own heart, took out a piece of himself, and placing it into the Man-shape, and blew his own life into his nostrils. Oh, the love in the heart of God for this creation! As the breath gave life, God reached down and pulled the man to his feet, where he was embraced by the Lord.

The man who was made in the image of God, who looked just like Him, who had the face of the Man!

18

Blazing ice-fury shook Lucifer, and looking at him, we saw pure evil. Nothing in Heaven had ever been like this before. He beckoned a grey-bound angel to come over, and then told the angel to find Abaddon, and tell him that the master had need of him.

"Master now!" Carbuncle remarked bleakly.

Abaddon rushed in. "You wanted me, Lord Lucifer?" Lucifer smirked. "Lord Abaddon, now I have seen what is happening, I have a much better plan. Tell the others to stand down. Convene a meeting for after this creation is finished, and I will explain. You are free to go now, *Lord* Abaddon."

"Did you hear that," I signalled the other stones. "Now he's calling Abaddon, 'lord.' What an atrocity!"

Our attention was brought back to creation, by a rush of angels taking flight toward the earth, for God had led man to that garden in the east. Lucifer had been correct. I recoiled at all we had heard, and how it was going according to Lucifer's plan. I had never felt lonely before, but now I was questioning myself, questioning all we had ever been taught. Diamond felt my confusion and answered.

"The Lord is God. He is immovable. Regardless, my fellow stones, though He slay us, yet will we praise Him," and I bowed in my heart to the glory of God, for He is God and I am not.

The Lord and the man reached the garden. "You are free to eat from any tree in the garden, but you must not eat from the tree of the knowledge of good and evil, for when you eat of it, you will surely die," He said.

The man nodded and understood.

Then, the Lord called all the animals he had created, to present themselves to the man, for he was to rule over the fish of the sea and the birds of the air, over the livestock, over all the earth, and over all the creatures that moved along the ground.

"Give each of these animals names," and the Lord stood aside to watch and see what the man would name them.

So many different creatures. And all of them with a mate, for male and female the Lord had created them.

"Cats," he said, as the great, soft-furred, four-legged beasts bunted and smooched around him. The man scratched the largest of the cats' heads, stroked the backs of smaller ones, and then bent down and picked up the smallest of the cat species, and put it on his shoulder. The small cat nestled into his neck, and gave a loud noise that the other cats picked up. Rumbling, rolling, purring.

Over and over, the animals paraded before him. "Horse," he declared, as a myriad of beautiful large animals with short hair, came to him. Some were striped; some had a rough coat and made a strange noise, a braying. Some looked as though they were half of the tall horse and half of the striped horse.

"Lama, Alpaca, Platypus, Armadillo, Mole, Giraffe, Camel, Dog."

"The ones that swing through the trees shall be called Monkeys, Chimpanzees, Apes."

Lumbering through to the central glade, where Lucifer had held that dreadful meeting, came the most strange of all. The man looked at these, from the very large to much smaller, and pronounced, "You shall be called dinosaurs."

The Lord God watched on. He was filled with great joy at this creation of man. When the parade of animals was finished, and they had left the garden, the Lord turned to the man and asked him if he had found himself a mate in any of the animals. "No Lord, there were none of my own kind there."

"No, there were not, and I wanted you to see that for yourself. For it is not good to be alone." And the Lord caused the man to fall into a deep sleep; and while he was sleeping, he took one of the man's ribs, and then closed up the place with flesh. Then, kneeling on the ground, the Lord God made a female of the man species from the rib he had taken from the man, and breathed life into her. Presenting her to the man, the man was overjoyed and said, "This is now bone of my bones and flesh of my flesh; she shall be called 'woman' for she was taken out of man."

The Lord God walked with the man and the woman in the garden, when the evening cooled, and talked with His children, mankind.

And He saw all He had done and said, "This is good."

As we watched, the seasons moved on, and we saw the same changes we had seen before, but this time when the trees budded with new life, so did the animals.

The birds that nested in the trees built nests and laid eggs, which hatched into young. The animals that wandered the earth grew heavy with child and when their time came, gave birth. All was as it had been created to be.

Gabriel called the delighted angels to order. When we finally brought our gaze back to this Heaven, we saw the Lord God, the Son and the Spirit of God had departed. Lucifer struck up a work of worship in which the whole of Heaven joined in. A masterful piece of subterfuge. For, if there had been any doubts as to his loyalty, he was not giving any ground to fuel them. To anyone looking on, he was a loyal angel, chief Cherub, and the one who walks in the stones of fire. Deceitful.

As the last refrain tapered off, Gabriel stood forward again.

"My brothers. We have seen such power and love exhibited from our Lord. This is the end of His creation of the Universe and this earth with all its inhabitants. We have seen a cycle of seasons with the new life being brought forth, just as God decreed. This is then, the sixth day and this is the completion of the heavens and the earth in their vast array. I bless you, brothers." And Gabriel stood back, thus ending this amazing time.

Time had been unheard of in Heaven before. The earth's seasons rolled through into each other; the heat of the summer with the beauty of the fall, followed by the biting cold of the winter. But the promise of the spring, brought hope for the future.

19

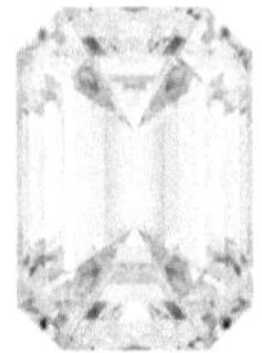

The angels watched, as every evening God would walk with the man and the woman in the garden in the east. The garden He had named, Eden.

The man called his wife, Eve, and himself Adam, for he was the first man, and from Eve would come life that would populate the earth with mankind, who would have such sweet fellowship, face to face with God.

At worship times, we would listen avidly to what the other angels were saying. "The Lord God talks to the Man and Woman about their roles in governing the earth." And another would say, "He is teaching them how to rule and reign, how to have dominion over the animals."

Each time, Lucifer would hear these reports, he trembled with rage. His countenance exuded such hate. How was it, that the other angels didn't notice?

And the grey robes remained – so many grey robes! The hardness and coldness of Lucifer's heart continued unabated.

Even in this, we nine stones were content to rest, for at least, it meant we could remain in the presence of God. The joy was palpable, angels dancing on the golden streets, flitting between Heaven and earth, rejoicing in God's love for this creation. It almost seemed that the previous conspiracy could be a bad memory, because nothing seemed to happen.

How often Lucifer and Abaddon met, we did not know, for he would now go out without his robe of office, and leave us on our garment rack in the music room. The house was again filled with the light of the Lord, with Virtuel remaining constant and honourable.

It seemed to us, that no matter how far he went from the heart of the Lord God, that Lucifer's gift for music remained. We had talked about it, and wondered whether that also could be corrupted? What would that look like? It was inconceivable that anything so wonderful, that brought all of Heaven to its knees in adoration, could possibly be used for evil.

As always, when Lucifer led Heaven in praise, my fellow stones and I reverberated the sound of Heaven. The vibrations of love filled us all and spilled over, with our colours reflecting off the presence of He who sits on the throne.

The deepest worship of my heart, was the silent reverent awe of the most High.

"Reign in me, Lord God. May your glory fill my whole being. May your presence never lift from me. For you alone, are the most High over all; You, who hold all of Heaven and the universe in your hand. How majestic is even your Name. Your presence overwhelms me, and I glory in your love." This was my heart's song and how I was, as we together with all the angels, bowed before the Three-in-One.

Cries of "Holy, Holy, Holy," resonated from all around us. The glory Presence pulsed, shining its radiance, illuminating and bouncing light off the Crystal Sea.

Deep in worship, I vaguely sensed sounds entering into my consciousness. Jasper jerked alert in silent alarm. Nine stones, snatched out from before the countenance of God, were being dragged by Lucifer, high up and over the angelic host, while he emitted a loud cry, penetratingly evil.

In terror, we looked down, where shouts and war cries could be heard, as angel battled angel. Taken unaware, as Dagon's troops, who had stationed themselves around the perimeter, sliced through the air, herding the angels at sword-point toward the centre of the sea. Incredulity met jeering taunts.

That which we had long hoped was forgotten, had begun.

Swords of light trysting with a maelstrom of wickedness.

We could hear the clashing of swords. The loyalist troops under Michael were prepared. Somehow, they had known and were hard behind. Pushing evil out, as light pulsed with power.

Michael was battling both Amon and Shemihaza. We saw Azazel, together with a squadron of warriors, heading towards the Halls of Justice, where Wisdom dwells. There was no sign of Abaddon.

As Lucifer tore toward the Throne, we saw Michael's sword of light pierce straight through

Amon who abruptly disappeared. Shemihaza dropped his sword and surrendered. Michael's troops took Shemihaza and his unit prisoners. We could no longer see Michael.

Disbelieving cries were heard from all over Heaven, and a tumultuous clashing of swords laid waste to the peace. Everywhere, swords of righteousness clashed with grey-robed angels.

War had broken out in Heaven!

Evil engulfed Lucifer. Nine stones shrieking with fear. In desperation, we cried to the Lord to save us. The noise from the war was so enormous, we knew He could not hear. Lucifer tried to make his break, ducking under Michael's sword, and flew toward the throne.

God had abandoned us. Through nothing we had done, we were now engulfed and by default, forced into treason. We were but a leaf, being carried away in a raging torrent.

Topaz grunted, as Carbuncle was flung against her. Lucifer zigzagged abruptly, and again twisted, so that we were thrown across one another.

Below us, angel battled angel, and those for the Lord started praising God, until the tumult of war was drowned out by shouts of "Glory to God in the highest. The Lord our God is our strong right arm. He is our righteousness, He is our victory." As the praises grew louder, it overcame the disharmony from evil, and the battle turned. The clubs and swords assailing the faithful, fell short of their targets. Through faith and praise, no weapon formed against the angels could touch them. Confusion fell on the aggressors, who turned on each other. Michael's warriors came from the rear, subdued and chained the enemy angels.

Lucifer's arrogance denied him knowledge. His one intent was taking the throne from God.

"MICHAEL!" Diamond positively screamed. All of Diamond's meaning came surging through, as a disperser of light to overcome, joined with Carbuncle's brilliance, as a flashing sword.

I could hear the roar of triumph as angels roared, "By the sword of the Lord and the Word of God, we have overcome."

Again, we were flung roughly together, while Lucifer tried to escape the net Michael had set, with his top warrior angels.

Thus, began a desperate tactical manoeuvring of Lucifer trying to get to the throne, with Michael and his angels fighting him. Desperation made Lucifer strong, but Michael held the sword of righteousness.

Seeing he was trapped, Lucifer turned to Michael. "My brother, think for a while. This is what the Lord God wants. Join us in this mission. He has appointed me as His regent, Michael."

Michael just looked at Lucifer with utter disbelief and sorrow. "Bind him and take him to the hall of justice." He instructed his angels.

Michael and his warrior troops fought against the dragon, Lucifer, and the dragon and his angels fought back. But he was not strong enough, and they lost.

It was over swiftly. One third of the angels were lost.

20

One third of Heaven's angels were brought to trial. One third of the angels were paraded in chains, before the rest of Heaven.

As they were marched down the Halls of Justice, Wisdom called out, "I, Wisdom, dwell with Prudence and find out knowledge. By me, do kings reign and princes decree justice. By me, princes rule. They who seek me, do find me. I lead in the way of righteousness, and in the midst of the paths of judgment."

Glaring at her, Lucifer was hustled forward to the judgment chamber.

Lucifer stood together with Abaddon and Amon. Behind them, were Dagon, Azazel and Shemihaza, with the rest of the accused gathered at the rear. Michael's warriors stood guard. The doors of the room were sealed. There was no escape.

Gabriel brought the court to order and read out the charges.

"God has given you over to your delusions and base nature. Did you really think you would succeed? Nothing is hidden from God's sight. Everything is uncovered and laid bare before the eyes of Him to whom you must give account. To whisper in one corner, is to shout in another. The Lord saw all, and heard all that you were doing."

Turning to Lucifer, Gabriel said, "You have been in Eden, the Garden of God. Every precious stone was your covering: Sardius, Topaz and Diamond, Beryl, Onyx and Jasper, Sapphire, Emerald and Carbuncle. The workmanship of your tambourine and of your settings was prepared in you in the day you were created. You were blameless and sinless. You resided in a different realm from man-to-be – on the mountain of God."

Gabriel paused for a moment. He was struggling, for Lucifer had been his brother. "Your heart became proud on account of your beauty, and you corrupted your wisdom, because of your splendour."

Silence reigned in the room. Faces resolute, the rebellious angels awaited their fate, as Gabriel continued, "The sin of your mouth and the words of your lips, have condemned you in your pride and your cursing."

Turning to Azazel and his troops, Gabriel went on. "You set off to get Wisdom, but Wisdom defied you. You were captured, and the guards surrounded and held you. Wisdom belongs to the Lord. Dagon, Shemihaza, and Amon, and the rest of you: The Lord has decreed that you shall be banished. You will never be allowed back into Heaven, nor ever again experience the glory of the presence of the Lord. Lucifer, together with all those who turned against the holiness of the Lord God, and made war in heaven - You are all to be banished."

Lucifer raged back at Gabriel, "I shall make war on man. They will worship me!"

Michael stood directly in front of Lucifer. "Even if you will not hear it, my soul weeps for your pride. The fear of the Lord is to hate evil, pride and arrogance. Pride goes before destruction, Lucifer, and a haughty spirit before a fall. Woe to the crown of pride." And he stepped back to allow Gabriel to continue.

"Abaddon! You saw the serpent the Lord God had created, and being a Seraph yourself, you saw the likeness. You entered into that serpent. Your sole purpose was to destroy mankind. You corrupted that which was pure and beautiful, to use for your own purposes. The Lord has pronounced judgment on you. You are to be thrown into the bottomless pit." Gabriel finished reading the charges.

There was a horrified murmur. Whispering afraid.

I started to scream. I'm sorry, but I couldn't help myself. Any control I had, was gone, for my eight brothers, sisters and I, being Lucifer's by right, were culpable. We were to be banished from the presence of God, and forever live in hatred and evil. At least, we stones would have each other, and though God cannot look on sin, we would do what we could to always worship Him. This deep time, screaming in anguish.

The room grew brilliant, dazzlingly bright, as the Glory cloud of God surrounded us. I drank in all I could, for this would be my last time to experience His love for me. I heard the fallen angels whispering to each other, "I cannot see the Lord!"

The Voice of Thunder spoke, addressing Lucifer.

"Do you not know that in me, you live and breathe and have your being? Shall a mere angel be more than God? More pure than his Maker?"

The condemned angel remained sullen, but the Lord continued, "I put no trust in the angels I charge with folly. You are condemned to be removed from my presence. You will be cast to the earth you are so jealous of. You will never know my Holy presence again, for I cannot look on sin. You were perfect in all your ways, from the day you were created, until iniquity was found in you. Your heart was corrupted by your vanity in your beauty. Beauty I made! You have defiled my Holy sanctuary. You have left your holy estate. Look at you, Lucifer! Once, you were the most beautiful angel. Now, look at each other, for the sin and evil that is in your heart, is now manifest on your face and beings. You have coveted my throne, but I tell you, Heaven is my throne and the earth is my footstool. You, Lucifer, are under my feet."

We were shrieking, as Lucifer was condemned. Horrified, I looked at Lucifer's face and saw nothing, but a great red dragon. Wildly turning to look at the rest of the condemned, they too had turned into hideous creatures. Their beauty was gone, replaced with corruption and cruelty. The light in their hearts had gone out, and Lucifer's music perverted.

"Now, I sentence you to eternal absence from my glory. You will be cast into outer darkness."

If I had thought that any of those angels would throw themselves on the Lord's love and mercy, I was wrong, for the evil in their hearts was too great.

Weeping bitterly, in absolute loneliness, I felt my life-force being squeezed out of me, as Lucifer sneered at God. The living flame inside me was dying. We were culpable in treason, simply because we were Lucifer's, serving the same fate as him. I felt very little and insignificant. My being was dwarfed by the selfish ambition of others. I had had a place and a purpose in the presence of God, and now, that was being stolen from me.

Yet, God wasn't finished. His presence grew more intense, and the condemned angels were driven to their knees. The Son came and stood right before Lucifer. Oh, how I loved the Son. I shone as brightly as I could, to let Him know: "Lord, I love you. I did not betray you. Though you slay me, yet will I praise you."

I would rather cease to exist, than to be separated from the Lord. My facets were fluttering and hope submerged. To be thrown into the same lot as Lucifer and the one third of the insurgents, caused shockwaves, resonating fright, and I cracked, broke in pieces, held together only by the gold setting. My very being was engulfed in choking, horrifying, panic. Suffocating life being extinguished.

"I believe you have something of ours, Lucifer. You shall not retain these." And thus saying, the Son ripped us, the covering garment, off Lucifer. The entire breastplate of honour.

Gasping, struggling to comprehend. Had we been delivered? I didn't understand. What was happening? Dawning comprehension, as the essence of love soothed my agitation. What great love was this?

The Son held us firmly. Rushing rivers of peace pouring over us. "Ssh. It's not quite over yet," He said quietly, and walked with great deliberation out of the chamber, and through the Halls of Justice, where Wisdom, Prudence,

Knowledge and Discernment watched with Justice.

Michael and his legions paraded the fallen angels back through the halls of justice.

Heaven waited in silence.

Lucifer and his leaders were the first. Marched to the edge of eternity, the great gates were opened.

All the angels, the twenty-four Elders, the men in white linen. All citizens of Heaven watched the dreadful spectacle. Great agony of hearts, as brothers watched brothers exposed in their atrocity, as they were made a show of, openly, righteousness triumphing over evil.

Lucifer was the first to be forced out of Heaven, where he fell, fell, fell, from eternity into time, to the earth he had so coveted.

Michael looked at the rest of the leaders and Michael's commanders forced them to the edge, where they, too, were thrown down. We looked in horror, as the one third of rebellion was cast out of Heaven.

And the gates of Heaven were closed against them.

Quietly, the Son returned to the City in the North. We could feel His heart. Such pain.

Coming into the presence of God, the full enormity of what had happened, swamped all nine of us.

"Lord!" Weeping, my broken heart being restored by His presence.

"My precious stones. Did you really think I would abandon you? I have seen your faithfulness. I have heard *all* your cries. I am so proud of you." The Lord held us close, God the Father, God the Son and God the Holy Spirit, were all present.

"Lord God, we called and cried for you. Why didn't you rescue us? Didn't you care about what we were going through?" Sardius, the one who shows her heart, asked the question we were all thinking.

The Son gently handed us to the Father, and walked back to His place on the throne. The Twenty-Four Elders bowed before Him. "Holy. Holy. Holy," rippled in adoration from those under and around the throne.

I glanced back at the Son, to tell Him just how much I loved Him, and was astonished at what I was seeing. For, He appeared to me as a lamb, kneeling there in complete beauty and absolute authority.

"I saw all that was happening," the Lord God said.

"Lord," I burst out, completely interrupting God Himself. "Why is the Son as a lamb?"

He smiled. The merriment in His eyes showed He had not missed that moment, and was enjoying my amazement.

"You will understand the Lamb someday, Beryl. Lucifer's plans did not take me by surprise, although he has manipulated and tricked Man into rejecting Me, their hearts are still soft toward me, and I have a plan to redeem them."

He was quiet for a heartbeat. Touching the Son on His shoulder, He said, "This is my Son, in whom I am well please. Behold the Lamb of God, who takes away the sins of the world."

The Lord God, The Son and the Spirit of God, for a moment, became as one and then as three again.

"You know that I have never left you, my precious jewels. I sent Virtuel to be with you and encourage you. I saw your faithfulness and courage, even when you were weak and thought you had failed me. I saw to it, that you would be in my presence in times of worship. I saw to it, that even when Lucifer's heart was far from me, that you were safe. Lucifer set himself against me, but I am omniscient, I am omnipresent, at all times in all ways. I saw all.

"I saw all that was happening," He said.

"But, Lord!" Diamond blurted, completely forgetting He is God, and we are not. "Why didn't you rescue us?"

"My precious stones. Even when you were at your lowest, your courage was recorded in the Holy Writings of Heaven, to give hope to many yet to come."

"I needed you to be proven, and to show your love and truth. Many will look at your example, and see all I have done and take hope. They will follow your example. You have shown the way forward for many. You have made a path, so mankind can see the way through their darkness and pain. Their path will be the same as yours; keep their focus on me. I will never leave them, I will never forsake them.

"Continue to praise me, for in those praises, my power to save is released. I will never ever leave them. No matter how dark the night is, I am always there, and there is always a purpose, even though they may not see it, until they reach eternity. Trust me."

Waves and waves of golden love and joy emanated from Him towards us. Tears poured down my facets. He had not forgotten me. There was design and meaning in all the pain, and I hadn't failed.

"My beloved stones, I am the master tapestry weaver. You can only see part of the tapestry. I promise you, one day, you will see it all. You will see the beauty I am weaving."

Gently, He reached out and touched me. I felt the occlusions clearing, and my facets returning to their brilliance.

"You did not fail, my Beryl. Fear not, for I have redeemed you. I have called you by my Name. You are mine. I will hold you close for a while, but your journey is not yet finished. There is more to come, as I prophesied over you all, when I created you."

"More Lord? What do you mean by that?"

"My little ones," the Lord God held us in His hand, "In the face of such great adversity, you remained faithful. Enter into your rest. Rest until the next journey, for there will be another mission."

Thus saying, He placed us directly into His beautiful heart.

After the horror of Lucifer, oh, the unutterable joy of returning to the presence and heart of God.

EPILOGUE

The great, red dragon faced down his council. He wore his best robes, gaudy and highly embellished, signifying what he thought of, as being his high estate.

"We lost that battle." He paused for effect, and glared at those in the council of the second Heaven. "But, we have the advantage of knowing God's vulnerability; His creation of Man. Therefore, that is where we shall hit Him hard; where it hurts the most." The viciousness in his voice, whipped those present. "We must destroy His creation, and this is how it will be done."

In palatial dark splendour, which housed the dank and icy headquarters, the Principalities, and Powers which ruled in unseen places, listened intently. Breath of sulphur and lava. Hot Fury. Vengeful. Hateful.

Those once known for reflecting the glory of God, once known as angels, now only reflected their own inner hatred. From beauty to sheer evil. From angel, to now known as a demon.

Shifting his crown aside to scratch his grotesque head, he paused for a while, and then continued. "For those who can be seduced into God-hatred, you have done your job. They are easy to control. We can corrupt them further. Those who insist on filling the God-shaped vacuum in their lives, fill it with idols. Idols of self or pride. Idols of money. Idols of false gods of wood and stone. And, for those who will not have either, fill them with lust for each other, perversion of all types. Any lust of anything, will work to our advantage."

Snickering, a maliciousness passed across his face. "Make man think that WE don't exist," he added, and broke into roars of laughter at that thought – that he, Lucifer, the great, was just a myth.

The once beautiful angel, who had been known as Lucifer, deliberately stopped speaking, looking at the evil demons before him. Each one of them, feeling the hatred emanating from those eyes.

Lowering his voice several octaves and whispering, he walked around behind the demons. "Of course, there will always be those who refuse to betray God," he spat the words out. "These are the ones we must compromise, in any way possible. Lead them into having a form of godliness, but tie them up with so many laws and rules, that they will be powerless to be who they really are." His words delivered in hateful ugliness.

"Kill them with a form of religion, which denies the power of God. Blind their eyes and deafen their ears to truth. Cause them to follow man, and not the Spirit of the Lord God. You must completely crush the true believers."

"But!" and he leaned forward to emphasise his point, "But. There will always be a remnant, and they are the ones to watch carefully. If you cannot entice them to partake in immorality, then use other believers to destroy them, through gossip and slander. Raise up powerful leaders for them to follow." He smiled maliciously. "They will play follow the leader, instead of following the Lord."

"It is *absolutely essential* that we capture the entirety of mankind, for God WILL have a plan to redeem them. Failure will not be tolerated. There is always the abyss…"

A corporate shudder swelled the room, at the mention of 'abyss'.

"I will be following this very closely, to ensure his plan of redemption is aborted. We cannot allow all we have worked on, to be destroyed. WE are the destroyers." Satanic stench fouled the air. Evil, rasping tongues.

Reaching out tentacles of enticement, weaving webs of deceit, the council gathered together, centring on regions of the earth, working on strategies to inflict the most damage. War. Hatred. Envy. Division. And, complacency with apathy.

Lucifer continued, "By lust, entice mankind to all kinds of perversion and deviancy, of that which is most pure – the love between the man and the woman. Entice man to mate with us! We shall destroy God's very bloodline."

The demons stopped their babble and listened, as the dragon turned to face the Princes of powers of the air. "We, the council, have discussed this, and plans for the destruction of mankind have been made in this matter. According to the laws that the Lord God Himself put into place, we, the princes of hell, own mankind, and we have every legal right to destroy them. So be it. Sabotage marriage. Ruin families. Pervert justice. Destroy His creation." Slowly, circling around the fallen angels, he continued, "We MUST ensure the bloodline is so corrupted, that no redeemer can ever be successful.

"Be the thief that comes to steal, kill and destroy. Council dismissed."

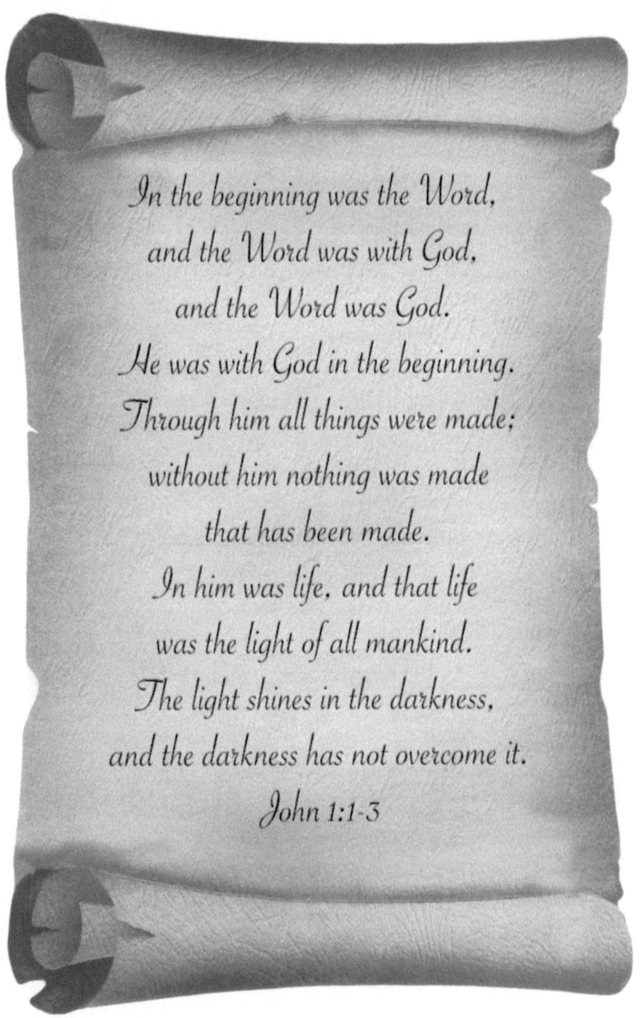
In the beginning was the Word,
and the Word was with God,
and the Word was God.
He was with God in the beginning.
Through him all things were made;
without him nothing was made
that has been made.
In him was life, and that life
was the light of all mankind.
The light shines in the darkness,
and the darkness has not overcome it.
John 1:1-3

APPENDIX

THE STONES

The Strong's reference numbers are included for your further study, as well as the Hebrew word used.

Sardius H124 Odem. אֹדֶם from H119 – feminine noun. Thought to have been a ruby or a garnet. Flows red. Blood red and speaks of sacrifice. Its name is made of two words: "Behold the son" and "Behold the Lamb of God." Ruby is therefore, The Son, or the Word's heart. He, whom we know as Jesus.

Topaz H6357 Pitdah פִּטְדָה- feminine noun. May have been chrysolite. Means to be pure. Loses its polish, if not cared for properly. The root word, means to be a stumbling stone. Of a pale yellow colour. Derivation of "building stone." Found in Ethiopia.

Diamond H3095 Yahalom. יַהֲלֹם from the root of H1986 – masculine noun. Hardness, to smite, strike, hammer, strike down, conquer, overcome, disperser of light, immovable. Where Diamond is mentioned, scholars generally agree that it would not have been a diamond as we know it.

Diamonds were tools, not precious stones, so we do not know what this stone really was.

Beryl H8658 Tarshiysh. תַּרְשִׁישׁ Probably of foreign derivation. H8659 – Masculine noun. Wise, to be pure. To be broken in subjection. Thought to have originated in Tarshish, a city in modern Spain, situated between the two mouths of the river Baetis (now Guadalquivir). Tarshish/Tartessus. The root word of Tharshish indicates yellow Jasper, however Scripture already gives Jasper on the breastplate.

It would be unlikely there would have been two Jaspers. Other scholars have suggested Amber, but that is then contrary to Exodus 28:20 and 39:13.

Onyx H7718 Shoham שֹׁהַם – masculine, resembles a human nail. Zeal for Yahweh. From an unused root, meaning 'to blanch.' J.D. Michaelis supposes it to be the onyx with whitish lines, comparing the Arab of 'a striped garment.'

Jasper H3471 Yashepheh יָשְׁפֵה – masculine noun. From an unused root, meaning to polish, be smooth. Yahweh is our strength.

Sapphire H5601 Cappiyr סַפִּיר – masculine noun. Sometimes translated as Lapis Lazuli. From the root word of H5608, a gem used for scratching other substances. Abrasive, used for scratching other surfaces, beauty and splendour. To be counted, taken account of, reckon, declare, count exactly or accurately. To inscribe letters on a stone, hence 'to write.' Chaldean in origin.

Emerald H5306 Nophek נֹפֶךְ – masculine noun. From an unused root word meaning to glisten, shining, symbolizes royalty, eternity, prosperity, Mercy, praise. To heal. Imported from Tyre. Could also be Turquoise

Carbuncle H1304 Bareqeth בָּרֶקֶת – feminine noun. Root word H1300 Baraq. Also, Emerald. Means flashing, bright, making a noise, thundering, comes from the notion of light. Lightning flashes, arrow-head. Applied to the brightness (glittering) of a flashing sword. The law of Yahweh, the Holy Scriptures.

HEBREW WORDS

Jehovah Sabaoth. H3068 & H4519 צָבָא יְהֹוָה - The Lord of Hosts, God of the armies of the stars, God of the unseen armies of Angels. Under the leadership and protection of Jehovah. Look also at H6633

El Elyon. H410 & H5945 עֶלְיוֹן אֵל 'El' refers to God. This is the shortened form of H430 Elohiym אֱלֹהִים. Usually rendered in English as

'God most high.' It occurs in Genesis 14:18-22 in the Masoretic text, and again in Psalms 78:35, 56. Psalms 57:2

Kabod. H3519 כָּבוֹד - Glory, abundance, honour, riches, splendour, dignity, reverence. See also H3513

Shekinah. - Glory. The glory of the Divine Presence, conventionally represented as light. A dwelling or settling place of the light of glory of God. The Semitic root means 'to settle, inhabit, dwell.' From the International Standard Bible Encyclopaedia: she-ki'-na (shekhinah, "that which dwells," from the verb shakhen, or shakhan, "to dwell," "reside"): This word is not found in the Bible, but there are allusions to it in Isaiah 60:2; Matthew 17:5; Luke 2:9; Romans 9:4. It is first found in the Targums.

Ruach. H7307 רוּחַ - Hebrew word meaning wind or spirit. Ruach ha Kodesh is used as the divine voice, referring to the Spirit of God or the Holy Spirit. See also H7306

Ikisat. H8314 שָׂרָף- Seraph/Seraphim, from the Hebrew meaning 'the burning one.' Isaiah 6: 1 - 8 used the term to describe six-winged beings that fly around the Throne of God, crying, "holy, holy, holy." Appears in Numbers 21:6-8, Deuteronomy 8:15, and four times in Isaiah 6:2-6,

Isaiah 14:29, and 30:6. They are mentioned in the Apocryphal book of Enoch, and again in the book of Revelation. The fallen Seraphs are seen as a poisonous serpent, which is why I think that the serpent that tempted Eve, was actually a Seraph.

Abaddon. G3 Ἀβαδδών- Revelations 9:11. And they had as king over them, the angel of the bottomless pit, whose name in Hebrew is Abaddon, but in Greek he has the name Apollyon. Abaddon means ruin or destruction. The name of the angel prince of the infernal regions, the minister of death and the author of havoc on the earth. See also H11

FOUR FACES OF THE CHERUBIM

Ox. H7794 - shōre - for ploughing, for food, as a sacrifice. When Jesus died, after three hours of hanging on that cross, he had no blood left. When the Roman soldier stabbed the spear into his side, he poured nothing but water. This was all after carrying his own cross piece of about 30kg for over a mile.

Lion. H738 - ar·ē' - images of lions, in the sense of violence. See also H717. When Jesus was beaten, it was so horrific that his face was lacerated, and beard ripped from his face. Then he had one nail cruelly hammered through the arches of both feet, and into the upright post of the cross. His arms were nailed to the cross section. One nail through each wrist, through the bone.

Eagle H5404 neh'·sher - From an unused root meaning to lacerate. Jesus was whipped and beaten. The whipping was so severe that it tore the flesh from his body.

Man - Sometimes translated as the face of a Cherub. Man is created in the image of God.

I find it incredible that God, whilst creating the Cherubim, foretold Jesus' death, way before Lucifer rebelled.

Jesus was the Son of Man. He was violently (Lion), lacerated. 40 stripes on his back (eagle), and then as an Ox, was slaughtered for the sacrifice. This then gives more understanding to Revelation 13:8, KJV, 'And all that dwell upon the earth shall worship him [the beast], whose names are not written in the book of life of the *Lamb slain from the foundation of the world.*' (Italics mine).

ON DINOSAURS

Microraptor; "Grey and brown body, with a short fuzz covering, with a long pale yellow bill and a comb on its head, the colour of the deepest ocean."

Plesiosaurus: "Did you see that enormous one with the long neck and small round head. It was comical. Such a round body and a short tail. Four flippers!"

Quetzalcoatlus: "immense birds with considerable wingspans"

PLANETS, STARS AND CONSTELLATIONS

Mazzaroth, Arcturus, Great Bear, Ursa Major, Orion. All the references are taken from the book of Job, Chapter 38

SCRIPTURES USED

Great Red Dragon. Revelations 12:3

Great Cloud of Witnesses. Hebrews 12:1

Seven Lampstands. Revelations 1:12, 13, 20;

Revelations 2:1.

Rainbow. Revelations 4:3. Revelations 10:1.

OTHER

Magnum Opus. A great work; especially, the greatest achievement of the artist. Merriam Webster Dictionary

JUSTINE'S LAST WORD

It has been a privilege to live with Beryl for the last year. As I have watched Beryl's response to the incredible drama he and the other stones were forced into, through no fault of their own, I have learned so much.

The Lord has changed me through the stones' journey, and I pray you will find the same courage that the stones found, for it is only as we lay ourselves and our own desires down, that we truly break through into His glory.

We are faced constantly with choices as the stones were. It is these choices that determine our next few miles in life, or in some cases, the rest of life.

It is my prayer that you will see the stones' choice to praise God, no matter the cost or consequence, as your own future.

Contacts:

theauthorjustine.wordpress.com

facebook.com/theauthorJustine/

or email at: theauthorjustine@gmail.com

ABOUT THE AUTHOR

Jesus is the centre of all that Justine is. She is a revelatory prophetic writer, who is passionate to see the Church in her rightful place in Christ. With a lifetime of knowing the Lord, her inner strength and under-standing of the things of God, shows in her daily interactions with others.

Justine and her husband, Stan, live in Auckland, New Zealand, together with their two crazy cats. They have two adult daughters.

NOTES

www.ingramcontent.com/pod-product-compliance
Ingram Content Group UK Ltd.
Pitfield, Milton Keynes, MK11 3LW, UK
UKHW040005200726
13854UKWH00001B/56

9 780473 451950